Breda's Island

JESSIE ANN FOLEY

Quill Tree Books
An Imprint of HarperCollinsPublishers

Quill Tree Books is an imprint of HarperCollins Publishers.

Breda's Island

Library of Congress Control Number: 2021953163
ISBN 978-0-06-320772-1

Typography by Kathy H. Lam
Map art by Torborg Davern / Shutterstock
22 23 24 25 26   SB   10 9 8 7 6 5 4 3 2 1
❖
First Edition

For Denis

Mair, a chapaill, agus gheobhaidh tú féar.

Live, horse, and you will get grass.

—Irish proverb

MAP of IRELAND

Dublin

DINGLE PENINSULA

Dún Chaoin

Dingle

Inch Beach

Blasket Islands

I.

JUNE

IT WAS HARD TO BELIEVE, AS THE PLANE touched down in a country Breda had never been, to spend the summer with a relative she'd never met, that this whole disaster was happening because of a stupid gym uniform.

Well, technically, it wasn't *just* the gym uniform. It was also a tiny crystal frog from Nuala's house, a set of neon gel pens from the art supply store, and a king-sized Snickers bar from the checkout line at Target.

And those were just the times she'd been caught.

She knew it was wrong to steal, of course, and she knew it only made her feel good for the thump of a heartbeat before making her feel utterly horrible for much, much longer. Worst of all, she knew how furious it made her mother. So why did she keep doing it?

"Simple, Mrs. Moriarty," the butt-faced principal, Mrs. Pope, had explained to Breda's mom that morning in May, glaring over her neatly organized desk while Breda squirmed. "The girl does it for attention."

"Em—sorry," her mom began to reply. "I'm not sure if—"

"Oh yes. Even negative attention is still attention, Mrs. Moriarty."

"It's *Ms.*, actually. There is no *Mr.* Moriarty in the picture, thank you very much."

And despite her situation, Breda found herself holding back a smile. Mrs. Pope knew how to make just about anyone feel stupid, but only someone like Breda's mother, who'd dressed up for the meeting in her best turquoise tracksuit with acrylic nails painted to match, had the power to make Mrs. Pope feel stupid right back.

Then again, maybe Mrs. Pope was right—maybe Breda *did* steal for attention. At school, she was neither popular nor unpopular: she was nothing at all, which was worse. And over the course of seventh grade, with her mom working around the clock to get the salon up and running, Breda had become nearly as invisible at home as she was at school. Some nights, she'd eat a sleeve of Girl Scout cookies for dinner, washing it down with a can of Coke, because her mom wasn't around to reprimand her about cavities or the nutritional needs of growing children. That was fun, at least until the stomachache kicked in. Other nights, she'd ride her bike around the city long past sundown, knowing that her mom wouldn't be home to fret about her and ask where she'd been. That was fun, too, at least until the loneliness kicked in. One week, she might keep her bedroom immaculately clean, and the next she could leave pizza crusts on her nightstand and hang her dirty underwear off the blades of her ceiling fan; it didn't make a difference—her mom didn't notice either way. So as much as she hated that the evil Mrs. Pope could be right about anything, Breda had to admit: it was very possible that her stealing *was* a cry for attention—after all, she didn't even *like* Snickers.

The gym shorts were different, though. *That* was a crime of necessity.

After the crystal frog, which Breda's mother forced her to return along with a homemade batch of "apology brownies," Nuala had placed the trinket back in its rightful place on her kitchen windowsill between the polar bear snow globe and the Waterford crystal paperweight. Then she'd hugged Breda and said, "Water under the bridge, pet—we all have our little rebellions when we're young."

Her mother, of course, had a different opinion. On the tense car ride home from Nuala's, she'd warned, "To steal from

Nuala—*Nuala!*—after all she's done for us? From now on, if I ever catch you stealing so much as an extra salt packet from McDonald's, I swear I'll send you off to spend the summer on your granda's farm. He'll straighten you out, so he will."

Breda knew this wasn't an empty threat. One of the things she liked the most (and the least) about her mother was that if Maura Moriarity said she was going to do something, she did it. Like the moving to America thing. Or the opening her own beauty salon thing. Or the no phone until you start eighth grade thing. It didn't matter that Breda had never even *met* her granda, that he had never so much as sent her a birthday card, or that they only spoke to him once a year, on Christmas Day, a brief phone call that always ended with Maura pouring herself a huge glass of Baileys over ice and glaring into the fake fireplace until the tears that trembled at the ends of her lash extensions melted away back into her eyes: Breda knew her mother wasn't bluffing.

He'll straighten you out, so he will.

And so, terrified at the idea of being shipped away to spend her summer with a grouchy old stranger, Breda kept her promise.

For a while, anyway.

But then, one morning near the end of seventh grade, she woke up with an ache in her belly. She ate a slice of dry toast for breakfast, which helped for a little while, but later that morning and all through lunch, the pain got worse and worse. She should have known what it was—she'd read enough books on the subject to know what to expect when the time finally came—but she didn't, not until gym class, when she snuck away from her pickleball scrimmage to use the bathroom and saw the smear of blood in her underwear. "Help," she had whispered, looking around the metal stall in a panic. But it was too late—the blood, Breda was horrified to discover, had already seeped through to her white gym shorts. How long had it been there? Had she been running around with a crimson stain on her butt, bending down, chasing after pickleballs, for the entire class? Had Layla Garcia, the most popular girl in school, who wore green contact lenses and had probably been using tampons since fifth grade, noticed? Had one of the other girls in Layla's clique? Or a *boy*? Why hadn't anyone bothered to tell her? Because it was more fun to laugh about it behind her back?

Lacking any real supplies, Breda had stuffed her underwear with wads of toilet paper, changed back into her regular clothes—silently thanking her morning self for choosing black jeans to wear to school that day—and hid out in the locker room until the bell rang. She made it through the rest of the day, shuffling slowly from P.E. to math to language arts so as not to dislodge the toilet paper situation in her pants. When she finally got home to the little house that always smelled of hairspray and ham, she had scrubbed vigorously at her gym shorts with a stain stick before tossing them into the washing machine with extra bleach. But when she took them out of the dryer, the stain was still there: it had simply faded to a hideous rust color so that now, instead of looking like blood, it looked like diarrhea.

She thought about asking her mom, a person who worked with chemical hair dyes for a living, for help in removing the stain. Ever since they'd gone to Target to buy Breda her first bra in sixth grade, her mom had been speculating about when Breda would get her first period. "First come the boobs," she'd proclaimed loudly as she dug through the racks of undergarments, her fake nails clacking against the hangers, "and next comes the blood." Well, now the blood had arrived, and Breda knew her mom would expect to be the first to hear about it. And maybe if this was still sixth grade, Breda would have told her. She could imagine it: how her mom would have doted on her, welcoming her to womanhood with a heating pad and a dose of Midol and a big pack of maxi pads. How they would have snuggled on the couch together, eating Irish chocolate and watching terrible Bravo television, and how it would have been an awesome end to an awful day. But as she stood before the washing machine, examining her ruined shorts, Breda felt a sudden wash of anger. Now that her mom owned her own salon, Breda practically had to pencil appointments into the calendar just to hang out with her. Sometimes she felt like just another client, instead of Maura's only child. Maybe her mom didn't deserve to know things about Breda anymore. Maybe another part of becoming a woman was having secrets. After all, her mother sure had plenty.

So, Breda didn't tell her mother. Instead, she shoved the shorts to the bottom of the garbage bin, beneath that day's breakfast dregs. She swiped a handful of pads from the giant basket of women's products her mom and Nuala kept for their clients in the silver-mermaid-wallpapered bathroom of their salon, and hid the stash underneath her bed. And the next afternoon, she slunk away from lunch five minutes early and went to the gym, where she stole Bella Martin's pristinely folded white shorts from the locker that Bella never bothered to lock. Bella, with her Apple Watch and designer water bottle, who owned three sets of gym uniforms because, she had once sniffed, it was *disgusting* to have only one, like Breda did, because that meant you had to stew in your own sweat for five days in a row. To be honest, as she was getting ready to commit the crime, Breda didn't even feel all that guilty.

Until Coach Nelson caught her in the act.

The very next day, after their meeting with Mrs. Pope, Breda's mom gathered up Breda's birth certificate and other important documents and dragged her straight to the post office. When she tried to protest, to beg her to reconsider, her mom just shrugged. "You know me better than that," she said. "When I say I'm going to do something, I do it." The line for new passports was over an hour long, but Breda had no choice but to wait next to her mother in sulky silence until her named was called, her stomach aching and a fat maxi pad stuffed between her legs.

The final month of seventh grade sucked worse than the first eight months combined. As it turned out, there was something even more terrible than being invisible. Now Breda's classmates actively hated her. The letter of apology Coach Nelson and Mrs. Pope had forced her to write Bella Martin had only made everything worse. What had they expected? Adults truly knew nothing about life. Breda wrote the letter in the principal's office, under Mrs. Pope's watchful eye, then placed the envelope on Bella's desk right before lunch. Bella made a big show of unfolding it, reading through it quickly, ripping it into four neat quarters, and then sashaying to the recycling bin to toss it away. As she strutted back to her seat, she sent Breda's yogurt flying off her desk with a quick hip check. All through the classroom, kids began hooting and clapping; phones were whipped out in case a fight broke out. But as Breda bent down to sop up her exploded yogurt, she felt for the first time a quiet kind of excitement about her summer banishment to Ireland.

True, Granda was a stranger, but he was still her grandfather, which meant it was his job to love her, whether he wanted to or not. Which was a lot more than she could say for her thirty-one classmates at James C. Palmer Middle School, all of whom now hated her guts.

A couple of weeks after the yogurt incident, the final bell rang, closing the book on Breda's seventh-grade year forever. Her mom picked her up in the school parking lot and brought her straight to the airport. As Breda headed toward the departures gate, her brand-new passport clutched in shaking hands, she set her shoulders firmly, determined to make the best of the unknown summer ahead.

2.

A S SOON AS BREDA, BLEARY-EYED AND sour-mouthed, deboarded the plane in Dublin, an air hostess (this was one of her mom's weird phrases; *nobody* else called them that!) met her at the end of the walkway.

"Slán, Breda, and welcome to Ireland!"

It was six o'clock in the morning Irish time, and all the passengers looked like zombies. But this woman, with her sparkly gray eye shadow, candy-pink lipstick, and fake bun pinned to the back of her head (Breda could recognize synthetic hair from a mile away; she hadn't learned nothing growing up in salons all her life), appeared to be totally immune to jet lag. If her mom was here right now, Breda knew the two women would be having an animated discussion about the benefits of thickening versus lengthening mascara. But, of course, she was not here: and Breda, barely off the plane, felt her first stab of homesickness.

"I'm Evelyn, and I'm an airline ambassador! My job is to make sure you find your way safely to customs. Would you like me to carry your bag for you?"

"No thanks." Breda tightened her grip on the handle of her duffel bag, as if this sophisticated, attractive woman, and not Breda herself, was the one with the reputation for stealing.

With a pleasant shrug, Evelyn turned on one of her low heels and led Breda down a wide gray hallway. Breda tried to keep up, shifting her bag from shoulder to shoulder. She'd been terrified the airline would lose her checked luggage, so she had stuffed nearly all her belongings into her duffel, and now as she carried it through the endless corridors, it felt like she'd packed it with lead weights. By the time they arrived at the customs line, she was sweating and the muscles burned all up and down her arms.

"This is your queue, love." Evelyn pointed to a sign that read NON EU CITIZENS. "Would you like me to wait with you?"

"Nope." Breda glared ahead.

She knew she was being rude, but people—mostly families in vacation wear—were looking curiously at the poor lonely girl being escorted through Dublin Airport by an "airline ambassador." If her mom didn't think Breda could handle the task of walking by herself out of an airplane and through a customs line without getting lost, then why did she think Breda could handle a whole summer living thousands of miles from anyone she'd ever known?

Evelyn, at least, seemed to get the hint. She politely wished Breda good luck and drew away, leaving Breda alone at last, clinging to her belongings and staring at the inflatable pillows still encircling the necks of the sunburned couple standing in front of her. She wouldn't be alone for long, though. As soon as the customs officer brought down his stamp upon her open passport with a *thump*, and she'd finally yanked and dragged her bag through the turnstile, there he was, waiting for her on the other side. He was dressed in a canvas work jacket and a pair of paint-splattered boots. A newspaper was folded under his arm. He had a full head of thick silver hair, neatly combed and parted at the side. His face was wrinkled and leathery, browned by decades of farmwork, rippled and sagging all over but with eyes that were stunningly ice blue, like a young man's, bluer even than the photographs, which were the only way she recognized him.

"Hi, Granda," she said.

"He better not try to hug me," Breda had grumbled to her mom in the car on the way to the airport. "Don't worry," Maura had laughed. "He won't."

And he didn't.

Instead, he reached out to grab her heavy duffel bag, throwing it over his shoulder as effortlessly as if it were filled with Styrofoam peanuts.

"Well," he said, giving her the once-over before he turned on his boot heel and headed for the baggage claim, "if it isn't my granddaughter, the thief."

3.

GRANDA DIDN'T SEEM TO BELIEVE IN SMALL talk. And he definitely didn't mind awkward silences. Breda kept waiting for him to say something, to ask her something, *anything*, even if it was the standard grown-up question—"So, how's school?"—or something else similarly boring. But for the first hour of the drive, as she stared out the window at the roads leading out of Dublin, he didn't say one single word. If Breda could only work up the nerve, maybe *she* would have asked *him* a question or two. She certainly had a few in mind: How come you never came to visit us, not even once? Why does Mom cry when you call her at Christmas? Are you still mad that she left? Or the biggest question of all: Do you know my father? And if you do, can you please at least just tell me his name?

Soon enough, the industrial buildings of Dublin's outskirts began to trickle away. They had arrived in the Ireland of wall calendars and thousand-piece landscape puzzles—hills in every shade of green; low, slow-tumbling clouds; sheep-dotted fields crisscrossed with hedgerow and limestone fencing. As a soft rain began tapping at the windshield, Breda's eyes grew heavy. She lapsed into a dreamless sleep, her mouth hanging wide open. When she awoke, wiping drool from her chin, they were just pulling out of a rest stop and back onto the highway. Even though it was only eight in the morning Irish time, Granda reached into the paper bag on his lap and handed her a tissue-wrapped cheeseburger. For himself, he'd purchased a paper cup of tea and a sausage roll. As the car filled with the scent of fast food, Breda realized how hungry she was—she'd been too nervous to touch the red clump of lasagna Bolognese she'd been served on the plane. She accepted the burger and took a massive bite.

"Wow," she said, chewing. "This is *delicious*."

"Tis made with good grass-grazed Irish beef. None of that grain-fed hormone and antibiotic-enhanced 'meat' you're used to eating in America."

Breda swallowed. She didn't like to think too much about what the cow she was eating had once eaten before it was turned into hamburger meat.

"How's herself, anyway?"

"You mean my mom?" Breda took another bite.

"The very one." Granda yanked the shifter into higher gear as they merged back onto the highway.

"She's fine."

"Mm."

Breda waited for a follow-up question—didn't all adults hate that meaningless adjective *fine?*—but it never came. The conversation had once again reached a dead end. It was two more hours to the farm, and in all that time, neither one of them said another word.

4.

I T WAS LATE MORNING BY THE TIME THEY
passed through Ballyglass, the village on the Dingle Peninsula that was closest to Granda's farm. There wasn't much to see: a post office, a couple of pubs, a gas station, an old stone church. The rain had passed, the fog had burned away, and the sky was clear and spectacularly blue.

A mile or so past the village, they approached a small white house, perched in the middle of a huge green field. As the car slowed to turn up the long paved driveway, Breda rolled down her window to stare. Granda's farm—her mom's childhood home—was stunningly beautiful, beyond what she had expected. The little white house had a blue door that seemed painted to mirror the color of the sky, matching wooden shutters, and a black slate roof that shone, still wet with rain. Behind the house were several outbuildings—white sheds with corrugated tin roofs, a long, low garage, and a small paved car park where a mud-splattered yellow digger was parked next to a pole hung with flapping laundry. Beyond the buildings, a steep hill rose up like a great green shelf. In front of the house was a huge sloping pasture that led down to the road. A herd of cows grazed there, their backs white as chalk in the sun. On the other side of the road stood a thatch of tall waving beach grass. Beyond it rolled the vast, lapping sea. As they came up the drive, Breda noticed that one of the cows standing near the wire-topped stone fence had a belly so swollen she seemed to sway from side to side, as if she would nearly tip over. When they passed, this cow watched the car with huge liquid brown eyes.

"What's that one's name?" Breda asked.

Granda glanced over at her. "Who's that now?"

"That one right there." She pointed. "The pregnant one. What's her name?"

"Is it the cow you mean?"

"Uh, yeah? Who else would I—"

She was now hearing his laugh for the first time. Rich and wicked and gravelly, it was her mother's laugh exactly.

"Sure we don't name the cows, Breda." He was still laughing.

"Tisn't as if they're pets. They're *livestock*."

"Oh." Breda's cheeks burned.

They'd pulled into the paved yard now. Granda twisted the keys from the ignition, and a small dog with shaggy white fur shot out from behind the shed, barking joyfully and jumping up and down in circles.

"That one, though," he said, still laughing to himself as he opened his door and patted the dog distractedly on the head, "you can call Jake."

5.

GRANDA GRABBED BREDA'S SUITCASE AND duffel bag from the trunk and Jake followed the two of them, paws clicking, into the little white house. The back door opened into a small, tidy kitchen that smelled of tobacco and fried sausage. Its pine-board cupboards, scored wooden table and chairs all looked like they had been built by hand, which gave the room a cozy feel, like a cottage in a fairy tale. On the wall above the table hung a calendar from a local car dealership, still stuck on April, and a framed picture of the Sacred Heart of Jesus. A tiny flickering lightbulb, meant to look like a real candle, was stuck in the middle of Jesus's chest. The red-tiled counter held a small old-fashioned radio, an electric kettle, a big cordless phone like the kind Breda had seen on nineties sitcoms, and a small plate crowded with several brown bottles of prescription medications.

"Cholesterol, blood pressure, the usual ailments," Granda said, seeing how Breda's eyes lingered on the cluster of bottles. "The blasted arthritis is the worst of it." He spread his hands out for Breda to examine. She hadn't noticed on the drive when they were curled around the steering wheel and gearshift, but now she could see: his palms were strong, thick as steaks, but his trembling fingers twisted off in varying directions, the joints puffy and purplish.

"Tis a devil of a thing, getting old," he said.

And Granda *was* old. Breda didn't know much about her family history, but once, at the salon, she'd overheard Nuala and her mom discussing how he hadn't met Breda's grandmother until he was already in his forties. Breda's mom was twenty-nine, which would make Granda seventy-something now. In other words: old. But he didn't *seem* old, at least not in the normal way, not in the way she'd seen other kids' grandfathers around school. Because even though his hands looked like they'd been smashed with meat tenderizers, and even though his face was as ridged with wrinkles as a wet shirt left to dry in the sun, Granda walked with a strong gait—a *stride*, almost—and when he removed his jacket and hung it on a hook next to the door, she saw through his thin cotton work shirt that his arms and shoulders were thick and ropy with muscle.

"Come on, then," he said, hoisting her suitcase. "I'll show you to your room."

The house was a bungalow, with all the rooms except the kitchen branching off either side of a long creaky hallway. They passed a small sitting room, a blue-tiled bathroom with a porcelain tub on rusting claw feet, and a closed door that Breda assumed was Granda's bedroom. At the very end of the hallway was the second bedroom, which had once been her mother's and, for the remainder of the summer, would now be hers.

The room was small and simple—the room of a farmer's daughter. Wooden headboard, wooden dresser, wooden nightstand, reading lamp, crucifix, a few sun-faded posters taped to the walls. Breda felt strange being there, like she was standing inside an exhibit from the museum of her mom's past—from those mysterious years before Maura Moriarity was a mother, before she was an immigrant. These were the sheets she had slept in. These were the posters she'd chosen to hang on her wall: Beyoncé. Westlife. The Blessed Virgin Mary. This was the trophy, perched on the windowsill, that she had won with her childhood team—*Ballyglass GAA Under-16 County League*

Winners—topped with a little bronze-brushed statue of a pony-tailed girl kicking a Gaelic football.

"You're responsible for your own laundry," Granda said, interrupting her thoughts. "The washing machine is in the shed. Clothesline is out back. Towels are on the toilet." He pointed to the little sliding door next to the bed.

Breda stared at the closed door. Did this mean what she thought it meant? Was she going to have her very own private bathroom for the whole summer?

"Tis not original to the house," Granda said dryly, seeing the excitement on her face. "I built it for Maura years ago. Her mother died when she was just a small child, and I indulged her, God forgive me."

He stepped aside, and Breda pushed open the sliding door. It was tiny, nothing more than a stand-up shower, a narrow sink, and a toilet, on the closed lid of which stood a stack of fluffy purple towels. It smelled a bit musty, and there were faint lines of black mold etched along some of the white tiles, but who cared? It was *hers*. No more hopping from side to side, nearly peeing in her pants, while she waited for her mom to finish up with one of her epically long showers. No more pushing aside her mother's huge bins of makeup, her buckets of brushes, her tangled cords of hot tools, just to be able to brush her teeth in the morning!

As Breda looked around, Granda pinched out his lower lip and stuffed it with a brown wad of tobacco. He then proceeded to explain, in great detail, the particulars of the home's water system. He showed her how to pull a metal chain hanging from the ceiling to activate the hot water for showers. Finally, without making eye contact, he warned her not to flush any "womanly things" down the toilet.

Breda pointed at the bulge of tobacco inside his lip.

"Did you know there are little bits of fiberglass in that stuff? It makes these tiny cuts in the lining of your gums and that's how the nicotine gets into your bloodstream. It causes mouth and tongue cancer eventually."

He stared at her.

"I didn't know they were after training twelve-year-olds to be medical doctors over in Chicago."

"I'm just saying, you should probably quit that stuff."

Granda responded by spitting a long stream of brown liquid into the paper teacup he'd brought in from the car.

"I don't come in here much anymore," he said then, looking around the little room with the cup clutched between his gnarled fingers. "Your mam's been gone a lifetime."

"Yes, *my* lifetime, technically."

There was an awkward silence. Breda knew very little about her mom's life in Dingle, the years before she'd come to

America. All she knew was that her mother had left home at seventeen, with Breda already growing in her belly, and that after she'd settled in Chicago, she had never returned home.

"Aye. Your lifetime." Granda cleared his throat and absently rubbed a thick palm across the smooth surface of the empty dresser. "Well, now. I s'pose I'll go make us some tea."

6.

THEY DRANK THEIR TEA AT THE KITCHEN table. Breda took hers with sugar and a splash of milk. Granda skipped the sugar but poured so much milk into his cup the contents of his chipped mug were practically white. Watching him, Breda smiled to herself. *The only thing my father and I have in common*, her mom often said, *is how we take our tea.*

He'd laid out a plate of Jaffa cakes, caramel digestive biscuits, and chocolate chip buns. Breda now understood where she'd inherited her sweet tooth from. They sat across from each other, chewing and sipping in silence while outside, through an open window above the sink, Breda could hear the occasional moo of a cow and the sough of the sea. A year ago, this kind of quiet meal might have made her uncomfortable. By now she was used to it, even if she still didn't like it. Over the past school year, her mom hadn't been around much—she was always working—but Breda could still remember having tea together when she was younger—the whirlwind of conversation, laughter, argument, gossip. So when the big cordless phone rang just as she and Granda were halfway through their cups, she was a little relieved at the interruption.

Granda scraped back his chair and picked up on the second ring.

"Hullo." He stuffed a whole Jaffa cake into his mouth and spoke around the crumbs. "Aye. She is. She was. She did. Twas grand. Grand. Grand. Grand, so. I'll put you on to her." He held out the phone. "Your mother."

"I'll take it in my room." She snatched the phone from Granda's calloused paw. She could feel him watching her as she hurried down the hallway. Maybe it was rude to leave him to finish his tea alone, but clearly, this was a man who was used to solitude. In fact, he seemed to prefer it.

"Breda, my love."

Just hearing the husky timbre of her mom's voice made Breda's eyes fill with tears.

"Mom." Her voice came out like a croak. She closed her door

and threw herself across the bed.

"Ah, pet. You're crying."

"Well, what do you *expect*?"

"The first days are the hardest, darling. I remember when I first came to Chicago—"

"Yeah, yeah. You ate nothing but 7-Eleven hot dogs because you didn't know how to work Nuala's oven and were too embarrassed to ask. I know, Mom." Breda wiped her eyes and readjusted the cordless phone, which felt gigantic against her cheek. "At least you came to Chicago by *choice*."

"Did I? Maybe you should ask your granda whether I came to Chicago by *choice*."

"Maybe I will."

Her mother laughed. "Let me know how that conversation goes."

"I can't believe you actually sent me away. Did you know Bella Martin got caught sneaking boys into her basement and her mom didn't even—"

"D'you really think I give the slightest you-know-what about what Bella Martin's mother does or does not do?"

"I'm just saying, you act like I robbed a bank! I only stole a couple things. *Little* things."

"Little or not, you gave me your word that you wouldn't do

it again, and you broke your promise. A woman's only as good as her word, Breda. And anyway, I can't have you breaking the law. That kind of negative attention is the last thing we want, and I don't think I need to remind you why."

"Do you even *miss* me? Or are you too busy with the stupid salon to notice I'm even *gone*?"

"So the salon's stupid now, is it? The salon that keeps a roof over our heads and food on our table?"

"I'm under a different roof now. Eating someone else's food. Thanks to you."

"No, thanks to *you*. Thanks to *your* actions. It's called personal accountability, Breda, and I've been teaching you to have it since you were in nappies."

Breda glared up at the posters on the wall. All of them—Beyoncé, Jesus's mother, all five members of Westlife—seemed to be staring at her. And perhaps because it was her mother's old room, they all seemed to be looking at her like they were on Maura's side. *Toughen up, kid* was what she imagined them saying.

"But Mom. He literally doesn't *talk*."

Maura laughed. "Oh, he'll talk. He'll roar and shout, too, if you give him cause. Trust me. How's my bedroom looking?"

"The same. Your posters are still up."

"You're joking."

"Nope. Granda hasn't changed a thing."

"Stop! What about my clothes? I left all my best stuff behind; I bet he binned it all—your granda never approved of the way I dressed."

"Hang on, I'll check." Breda got up from the bed, tripping over her unopened suitcase in the process. She pulled open the dresser drawers. They were all empty except for a few sachets of lavender, so old that the contents had turned to purple dust and contained barely the trace of a scent. "Nothing in the dressers."

"What about the wardrobe?"

Breda cradled the phone under her chin, found the two accordion doors against the wall, and pulled them open. It took some effort, because the closet was stuffed to the brim. Two starched school uniforms—blue sweater, gray pleated skirt, blue-and-gray-striped ties—were the first items on the rack. On the chest of the sweaters were sewn the words: *Scoil Reálta na Farraige*. Star of the Sea School. But the rest of the closet space was devoted to party clothes: tight miniskirts, cheap dresses with animal prints and thin straps, ripped jeans with rhinestone seaming on the butt pockets folded neatly over hangers—all over a decade old but still so completely, unmistakably, Breda's mother's style. Breda closed her eyes and leaned into the wall of fabric. It mostly smelled musty, but there were other secrets buried there, too, the wispy, eye-watering smell of cigarette smoke and the spicy, floral bite of Angel, the perfume that came in a huge glass bottle with a sharp cap that looked like a weapon. Her mother still wore it daily, spraying herself at all her pulse points, plus down her cleavage.

"Wow, Mom. It's all still here—all your outfits."

"You're *joking*. Well, feel free to borrow. Especially if you ever feel like testing out whether Granda is capable of roaring and shouting."

"Uh, no thanks." Breda ran her fingers along the slippery material. "And anyway, I'd look ridiculous in this stuff."

"Now, Breda. You couldn't look ridiculous if you tried."

Breda heard the phone rustle, could imagine her mom readjusting herself on their cheap gray futon, tucking her pedicured feet beneath her denim shorts, tossing her long hair, eyeing herself in the reflection of the turned-off television screen. She closed her eyes, but it was too late: two tears escaped and slipped down her cheeks.

"Mom, I gotta go."

"Already?"

Her mother sounded hurt, but Breda swallowed the lump in her throat. She was still supposed to be angry, even if all she really felt was sad. "Yeah, I should go help Granda with the tea dishes."

"Good woman, so."

"Bye, Mom."

"Wait—Breda."

"Yeah?"

"Before you go, there's something I should tell you. I should have mentioned it before you left."

"Okay. What is it?"

"Your granda has a—well, not exactly an affliction. More like a condition."

Breda swallowed, remembering all the prescription bottles on the kitchen counter. Down the hall, she could hear the hiss of water through the pipes, the clinking of glass as he washed the tea things.

"He tried to explain them to me once, when I was small. Night terrors, they're called."

"You mean nightmares?"

"Not quite. You know how, when you have a nightmare, you might dream that someone is chasing you, or something terrible is happening to you—like a horror movie?"

"Ye-es," Breda said slowly.

"Well, with a night terror, there is no plot. Only images.

The most terrible images you can imagine, and they are very, very vivid. I don't know how bad it is these days—maybe he doesn't have them at all anymore. But when I was growing up they happened all the time. Not every night but . . . often. The farm is so quiet, and when he's experiencing a night terror, he'll scream. And I mean *scream*. Tis a terrible sound, the way it rings throughout the house, and when he has one, tis difficult to wake him. But you *must* wake him, or he'll keep on screaming." She paused. "Do you think you can do that, love?"

Breda looked out the window at the wide green fields sloping down to the sea. Granda had no neighbors. Out here, there was no one to turn to if she ever got too afraid. "I mean . . . I guess I'll have to."

"The good news is that they're harmless. Probably more frightening for you than they are for him. I'm sorry, Breda. I should have mentioned it sooner."

"But why does he have them? Is it a medical thing or . . . ?"

"I've done a bit of googling. The internet says a traumatic past, a violent history, usually has something to do with it."

"Does Granda have a—a violent history?"

Breda's mom laughed, a puff of joyless noise. "Do you think he ever said a word to me about his history? He's an Irishman of a certain generation. He couldn't talk about his feelings if he tried. And believe me when I say that he *doesn't* try."

"Great. So you sent me away to spend the summer with an old man who doesn't talk during the day, but also screams in his sleep. Cool. Thanks, Mom."

"Ah, Breda, I told you: tis harmless. Just a little frightening for the listener, if she isn't prepared for it. Now, go on and help with the dishes. I love you, darling."

"You too."

"Me too, what?"

Breda sighed.

"I love you, too."

7.

AFTER BREDA HUNG UP, SHE WENT INTO her duffel bag and dug out the little moleskin notebook Nuala had given her to record her observations about her new surroundings.

1. We don't name the livestock

   she wrote.

2. Granda's hands look like old tree roots

3. He doesn't ever look at me, even when he's talking to me

4. What are the things he sees at night? Are they real monsters? Are they memories?

That was as far as she got before her mind began to wander. She tented the notebook across her chest, leaned her head against her pillows, and eyed the closetful of brightly colored clothing at the end of her bed. At the beginning of middle school, she'd thought maybe it would get her somewhere, being the daughter of the most beautiful mom at school. But in fact, it had the opposite effect. Maybe it was because Breda herself was awkward and mousy, skinny as a stick bug, with pimples that had started appearing on her chin and long, limp hair the color of a dentist's chair. But Breda knew that was only part of it. She knew, even though nobody had ever exactly said it, that her beautiful mother was the wrong *kind* of beautiful. When there were school assemblies, the other moms wore skinny jeans and soft, loose turtleneck sweaters or tasteful black yoga pants and sporty fleece vests. *Her* mom, on the other hand, wore padded bras beneath tight pink tracksuits. The other moms wore their hair in carefully messy buns or neat ponytails, but Maura had black roots and bleached-blond ombred hair extensions that fell all the way down her back and which she styled into tendrils with a smoking curling iron so that every morning, the whole house reeked of burnt hair. The other moms got short, neat manicures with neutral colors like "Ballet Slipper" and "Marshmallow;" Breda's mom had acrylic claws painted in primary colors and studded with rhinestones. The other moms wore lip gloss, maybe some mascara to pickup; Maura was never seen in public without a smoky eye, a matte lip, and a cloud of Angel so thickly applied that Breda had to insist they not hug each other before she left for school, lest she incite the nonstop sneezing of Dane Jackson, her desk mate, who had a fragrance allergy.

Worse, Breda's mom was always *saying* the wrong things. She cursed, for starters. Frequently and with gusto, in front of parents, teachers, and younger siblings alike. She called the bathroom *the bog* or, simply, *the toilet*, which was so gross and humiliating compared to the other parents' *powder room* and *restroom*. It went without saying that their little two-bedroom home, which they rented from an older Irish man who'd given them a good rate because he was in love with Breda's mom, was located in the wrong part of town. And while there were plenty of kids in school being raised by single moms, Breda was the only one she knew of who didn't even know who her dad *was*. Which had actually never bothered her all that much until Sophie Taylor's twelfth birthday party.

"Your mom couldn't make it today?" Sophie's mom had asked that afternoon when Breda came up from the huge basement, with its foosball tables and popcorn machine, to use the *restroom* and came across all the other parents sitting in the kitchen drinking coffee and chatting.

"No, she works on Saturdays," Breda had said.

"Too bad. She's such a hoot!"

"She *is*," agreed Mrs. Garcia, Layla's mom. "She's so salt of the earth, you know?"

Breda had nodded, even though she didn't know, not exactly.

"How old is she, anyway?" Mr. Wiemer had asked casually. All the parents were looking at her with glittering, expectant eyes.

"I don't know," she said cautiously. "Like thirty?"

The parents had all raised their eyebrows, glanced at each other across the rims of their coffee cups. It was clearly the wrong answer, even if it wasn't the truth: her mom was actually a little younger than that.

"I love her accent," said Mrs. Taylor. Then she added, smiling toothily, "Is your dad from Ireland, too?"

One of Maura's rules of thumb, which she had apparently learned from Granda, was this: *when in doubt, say nothing.* So in response to Mrs. Taylor's question, Breda just stood there in the middle of the adults, and stared at Sophie's mom until she cleared her throat and looked away.

"Well," Mrs. Taylor said, picking up her coffee and sipping it embarrassedly, "hopefully she can make it next time."

When her mom had gotten home from work that night, as soon as she'd kicked off her shoes, Breda had demanded, "Why didn't you come with me to Sophie's birthday party?"

"I was *working*." Breda watched as her mother threw herself, groaning, across the couch. "What's with the snit?"

"You could have taken off!"

"And, what, not paid our phone bill this month?"

"Everybody else's parents were there. Sophie's mom, Finn's dad, Layla's mom . . . *everyone*. You would have had fun."

"*Fun?* Ha! That Taylor woman looks about as much fun as my period."

"*Mom.*"

"*What?*" Her mother reached up and expertly twisted her long tendrils into a high bun, securing it in place with one of the hair ties she always kept around her wrist.

"I need to ask you something."

"Ask away, love."

"Was my dad from Ireland, too?"

At that, her mother gave a huge sigh. "Sure where else d'you think he'd be from? Timbuktu?" She flicked on the television. "Now do you have any other whingeing to do, or may I turn on *Property Brothers?*"

Despite her mom's many imperfections, Breda knew what nobody else seemed to know, not even her own granda: that Maura was a tough and kind and excellent mother. Wasn't that why Breda was here now in Ballyglass? *Personal accountability.*

How many other parents would have followed through on a threat like this? Certainly not Bella Martin's mom, or, for that matter, Sophie Taylor's. No matter how angry and hurt Breda felt, she had to respect her mother, too. She reached into the closet now and pulled out a dress with undulating patterns of zebra skin. She took off her jeans and T-shirt and quickly pulled the dress over her head, zipping it up the back. It was loose all over—Breda didn't have any of her mom's curves, at least not yet. She stood before the mirror that hung on the other side of the wardrobe and examined herself.

She'd been right, of course: in her mother's clothes, Breda looked absolutely ridiculous.

8.

BREDA WAS CHANGING OUT OF THE EMBARrassing zebra dress and back into her normal clothes when she heard the sound of conversation carrying down the long hallway. The gruff, musical cadence of Granda's Kerry accent and another voice, softer. A woman's.

Breda went into her (her!) bathroom and splashed some eggy-smelling water on her face, then scrutinized herself in the mirror. A pimple was burgeoning beneath the skin of her left cheek, and several more threatened along her forehead, thanks to almost-teenager hormones and eight hours of recycled airplane air. She dug through her toiletry bag, found her concealer stick (which her mom had bought for her on that same cringey bra-shopping trip to Target) and dabbed it on the reddening bumps. Then she ran a brush through her hair and padded back down the hallway in her socks to investigate.

"Hi."

Breda said it quietly, but the woman whooped, then whirled around as if Breda had just slammed a door with all her might.

"Breda! Tis really you!"

Breda couldn't respond before being crushed in a tight hug. The woman, whoever she was, was small and soft, with a round, kind face. She smelled a little bit like the dusty lavender sachets in the dresser.

"So lovely to see you at last!" She let go of the hug and squeezed Breda's arms. "I'm your granda's friend Noeleen."

Friend? Breda bit the inside of her cheek to keep from smiling. Did that grumpy old man have a *girlfriend*? She couldn't wait to tell her mom about this.

"You're very welcome here, Breda," Noeleen continued. "Your granda is so thrilled to have some company this summer. Aren't you, Davey?"

From the sitting room came a grunt. Breda glanced through the doorway. Granda was sitting in a leather recliner, his face hidden between the two opened pages of *Irish Farmers Journal*. Jake was asleep, his snout resting on Granda's socked feet.

"You must be absolutely starved with the hunger. I'm just about to put on the spuds. Why don't you go sit with Davey while I get everything settled?"

Breda glanced into the other room. The newspaper pages turned with a hostile flick. "Um—why don't I help you get dinner ready instead?"

Noeleen looked up, her face flushed over a pot of boiling water. "Not a'*tall*, my dear. You're a guest, and you must be absolutely *wrecked* from your travels. Now go on into the sitting room and sit with your granda. You two have loads of catching up to do."

Breda thought of arguing, but she could already tell from Noeleen's good-natured bustling that the matter was settled, and so, reluctantly, she trudged into the sitting room. Granda peeled off a section of the paper and handed it over without looking at her. Breda perched on the edge of the couch and skimmed an article. It was about price increases in the malt seed industry.

"Your mother."

Breda looked up. Granda's voice was muffled behind his wall of newspaper. She waited for him to go on.

"What'd she have to say for herself?"

"Oh, she just wanted to make sure I got here safe."

"She's still working at that beauty parlor, is she?"

"House of Hair? No. She actually opened her own salon with Nuala earlier this year." In her head she added: *How could you not know that?*

"Nuala. Nuala . . . remind me, is she your one from Galway? The one your mother lived with when she first went over?"

"Yes. That's her. Mom's *best friend*." *And you*, she added silently, *can't even be bothered to remember her name*.

"Tell me, then." He pulled the paper down with a crinkle and glanced at her over the tops of his reading glasses. "How did your mother manage going into business for herself, given her legal status?"

Breda shifted uncomfortably on the arm of the couch. She had been given very specific instructions to not, under any circumstances, discuss her mother's "legal status." You just never knew who could be listening. She thought of that day back in November, in social sciences class, the argument she'd had with her awful, pinch-faced teacher, Ms. Landry. Every Friday was current events day, and Ms. Landry was talking to the class about the immigration crisis at the Mexican border. "Did you kids know," Ms. Landry said, "that right now as we speak, there are over ten million illegal aliens living in the United States?"

"Don't call them that," Breda had muttered under her breath.

"Breda? Did you say something?" Ms. Landry was looking at her in surprise. All the kids turned and looked too, because Breda hardly ever spoke up in class. She hadn't meant to this time, either. It had just sort of spilled out.

"No," she said quickly.

"You did!" Ms. Landry crossed her arms over her lanyard and gave her an encouraging smile. "Please, share with us. We want to hear your thoughts!"

"It's just, um." She stared down at the doodles in her notebook, her cheeks blazing. "It's just that they're not aliens? They're, like . . . people?"

"Oh, Breda." Ms. Landry had laughed in that annoying voice adults sometimes used, the voice that says *I have diplomas and I'm smarter than you*. "That's just the term we use for criminals who come to our country illegally. Now, as I was saying . . ."

Breda continued to stare down at the stupid doodle of a tree she'd drawn earlier. Beneath her desk, she squeezed her fists tight. Her mother was not a criminal or an alien. She was just a person, trying to live a good life. Why had Ms. Landry demanded that Breda speak if she was just going to shut her down anyway?

When she'd gotten home from school that day, Breda had stormed straight down to the salon to tell her mom what had happened.

"She was so *rude* about it," Breda raged, while her mom foiled Joana, one of her most loyal regulars, who had emigrated from Romania five years earlier and cleaned houses for a living. "She just brushed me *off*. She seriously thinks there is nothing wrong with that term."

Her mom nodded as she crimped the foil around a chunk of Joana's hair.

"You know what I'm gonna do?" Breda said. "I'm going to send her an email tonight."

Her mom paused her foiling to glance over at her daughter.

"A *polite* email," Breda said quickly, noting her mother's face. "I'm just going to tell her that *not* everyone uses that term, actually. *Some* of us prefer 'undocumented immigrants.' It's a teachable moment, Mom!"

"You will do no such thing," her mother had snapped, brandishing her handful of foils. "You've already said far too much as it is."

"*What?* But I thought you said that when ignorant people—"

"I know what I said. I know." She dropped her hands to her sides, suddenly looking very tired. "But, love, you can't draw attention to our situation. Not ever. Right, Joana?"

Joana nodded sagely, her foils rustling. "Never," she agreed.

"Breda, all it takes is one angry client, or teacher, or school parent. One phone call. And all of this—our lives, everything we've worked for—poof. Gone."

Poof, gone. What she'd meant by that was jail, followed by deportation. They would lose the salon, all their money, all their savings. Being an *illegal alien*, her mom had explained, was like living in the crook of a slingshot—no matter how far

46

you stretched yourself forward, you could always be snapped back, in one violent motion, and end up right where you started.

"There are over ten million undocumented immigrants in the United States," Breda said now, answering Granda's question. "And lots of them have their own businesses."

"Hmph," he said. "You ask me, it's no way to live."

Yeah, well, she thought, *good thing I didn't ask.*

"And this 'salon'—how big of an operation is it? How many square feet? What are her overhead expenses? Is she earning enough to cover the rent?"

"I don't know the square feet," said Breda. "We converted our basement into the salon space."

"Ah." Granda lifted his newspaper again. "I see. My daughter, the big American CEO. Running her empire out of a basement."

Breda clenched her jaw. "She's doing really well with it," she said tightly. "You have to book a month in advance if you want an appointment."

"A month's notice for a bloody haircut?"

"Not *just* a haircut. She also does color, highlights, extensions, brow tinting, balayage—"

"Balayage? Brow tinting? I'm afraid you've lapsed into a foreign language now."

Breda glared at him. If he only knew how hard she, her

mom, and Nuala had worked to transform that dull concrete basement into the cozy little oasis it was now. The weekends they'd spent priming and painting the cinder-block walls a warm and tasteful mint green, the garage sale mirrors they'd brushed with gold paint that now hung above the workstations; the waiting area with the fashion magazines carefully fanned out on the coffee table, the secondhand couches her mom had reupholstered in soft pink velvet, the fluffy zebra-print throw pillows they'd chosen from HomeGoods. They'd bought cheap glass chandeliers from Ikea and hung them so that they cast a sparkling light across the whole space. And the floor! At first it had really stumped them. It was ugly and cold, unfinished concrete, but it couldn't be covered over in carpet because in a hair salon, you need a floor surface that is easily sweepable. Eventually, after a consultation with one of her mom's friends, who worked as a flooring contractor, they'd power washed the concrete and refinished it with an epoxy mixture that left it as smooth and shiny as an ice rink. It looked *so* chic, and they'd done it all themselves! So many times Nuala had wanted to hire somebody to help them with the work or the painting, and so many times Breda's mom had said no, it would mess with their profit margins, and anyway, she was a proud country girl whose father had taught her how to build, fix, and remodel just about anything. Maybe *that* would impress Granda, maybe *that* would make him proud, but as Breda sat and watched him grimly paging through his newspaper—crop reports, cattle prices, GAA scores—she decided it was no longer something he deserved to know. He didn't deserve to know, either, about all the women who came to the salon, who told their friends about it, who loved Maura Moriarity, not just because she was a good stylist but because she was good at making them feel beautiful, feel *seen*. He didn't deserve to know how Breda spent her weekends sweeping up their hair cuttings and shampooing out their color and massaging their heads with such loving care, these immigrant women from Ireland, yes, but also Mexico and Poland and Ecuador and Albania, most of them all too happy to pay with cash because their "legal status" was also not to be spoken of. Her mom and Nuala had built something really special—with zero help from anyone at all—and here was this mean old man, mocking it.

Well, if he wanted to play the silent card, so could she. She tossed her pages of *Irish Farmers Journal* onto the couch and walked out of the sitting room without another word.

9.

THE PLATES IN THE KITCHEN WERE SET and two ceramic dishes stood steaming in the middle of the table. One was piled high with potatoes, skins on, salted and buttered, while the other was filled with sliced boiled carrots and turnips. This was the kind of simple country cooking Breda got in Nuala's apartment, or at Irish Heritage Center Christmas parties. Noeleen handed her a large metal spoon.

"Serve yourself, pet," she said. "Don't be shy now."

Breda smiled and took the spoon, heaping her plate. As she waited for Noeleen and Granda to serve themselves, she watched a golden pat of Kerrygold melt into her potatoes, her mouth watering. She was about to dig in when Noeleen got up from the table to pull a third platter from the oven. The older woman set the platter carefully on a woven trivet next to the veg and peeled back the foil. And there, in the middle of the tray, was a huge pink slab of ridged flesh surrounded by lemon wedges. Breda's appetite evaporated. This was a very large, very expensive piece of salmon, she could see, most likely purchased specially for her arrival.

There was just one problem.

Breda *hated* seafood.

She hated how it smelled.

She hated how it tasted.

She hated the scales, still attached to one side of the fillet, that stuck to her mom's baking pans and that Breda had to scrub off with steel wool when it was her turn to do the dishes.

She hated that awful mealy, fleshy texture in her mouth.

Her mom used to force her to eat it—*it's packed with omega-3s!*—until one night, when she was eight, and she vomited it up all over the table. That put an end to that.

But now, here was Noeleen, sweet, kind Noeleen, who Breda had just met, sawing off a huge slab and dumping it with a wet *thwat* onto her plate. Breda knew the rules: when you're a guest at someone's table, you eat what you're served. So she looked at the lump of pink meat before her and tried to think of it as food, delicious, nourishing food, tried not to picture instead a cold, slimy tail or round, lidless eyes or, most horrifying of all, those huge black gills, flapping underwater like knife wounds that never healed.

It didn't work.

Granda and Noeleen were already concentrating on their own food, heads bowed over their plates. Maybe, Breda thought, if she ate all her veg, they wouldn't notice she hadn't touched the salmon. She got to work on the deliciously fluffy, buttery potatoes, nudging them to their own protected corner of the plate so they wouldn't be contaminated by the clear liquid oozing like pus from beneath the fish. When she looked up, though, Granda was staring at her with those ice blue eyes of his.

"What's the matter? Aren't you hungry?"

"I'm eating," Breda answered.

"Only the spuds. And spuds on their own are not a proper meal."

"I—"

"Are you ill?"

"No."

"Then eat your dinner, so."

If she were in her own home, Breda would have gotten up to pour herself a bowl of cereal. Or, no: she wouldn't be in this situation in the first place, because at home, her mom *knew* her, her likes and dislikes, her loves and hates. But home was five thousand miles away. She poked at the fish with the edge of her fork and waited for Granda to return his attention to his own food. Then she hacked up a few more pieces and pushed them around her plate. After a few minutes of this, she could feel him watching her again. This time, he placed his own fork and knife crosswise on his plate.

"Breda."

"Yeah?"

"Is there something wrong with Noeleen's cooking?"

"No." Breda smiled quickly at Noeleen, her cheeks hot. She stabbed a carrot. "Everything's great."

"Ah, now." Noeleen reached across the table and patted Breda's hand. "You don't like salmon, do you, pet?"

"Um." Breda glanced between the two adults. "I mean— sorry. It's just that I don't really like fish."

"She don't like *fish*?" Granda's jaw hung open, and his bright white false teeth flashed. "How can a child not like *fish*? I've never heard such rubbish in all my life."

"Lots of American children don't like fish, Davey. Some Irish ones, too." Noeleen met Breda's eyes across the table and winked. Breda smiled down at her plate.

"Bad enough that she's a thief; now she refuses a fine home-cooked meal? What are you, girl? One of them bloody vegans? I've some bails of silage out near the shed, would you prefer some of that?"

"Now, Davey——" Noeleen began.

"I'm not a thief." Breda's smile was gone now. "I did steal a few things, but it was stupid, and I'm done with that now. And I'm eating the veg, so calm down."

"Calm down? Did you hear that, Noeleen? The mouth on her!" He clicked his tongue in disapproval. "Briseann an dúchais, trí shúil an chat."

Breda didn't speak Irish, but she recognized the phrase because Nuala often said it about Breda and Maura: *Black cat, black kittens.* Like mother, like daughter. The difference was, when Nuala said it, she was speaking with affection. Here, it was a criticism.

"I guess my mother, *the big American CEO*, never taught me any manners," she said, picking up her fork. "But if you're gonna make such a huge deal about it, then fine. I'll try some."

"You will, indeed!"

She knew he was expecting her to take the tiniest bite possible, this American diva, this little kitten who'd come to Ballyglass to complain about everything and ruin his summer. So instead she did the opposite. She cut herself a gigantic chunk and boldly stuck the whole thing in her mouth, scales and all.

"Aha!" Granda sat back in his chair, smiling triumphantly as he crossed his brown, muscled arms across his chest and watched her chew. "An American child reared on McDonald's has finally tasted real food. Real, fresh-caught, wild Irish salmon. Tell me you've ever had anything better in all your life."

Breda forced herself to swallow, and even to smile back. She reached for her glass of water, and as the cool liquid spilled down her throat, her mind wandered, for the briefest second, to the exact place she had commanded it not to go. The gills, the tail, the lidless eyes. She tried to speak, but her mouth was flooding with saliva. She managed to push away from the table just in time, so that when it came back up, the puke splashed all over the floor and not the dinner table.

10.

B REDA DIDN'T REMEMBER FALLING ASLEEP. She remembered Noeleen helping her to her bedroom and digging a clean pair of pajamas from her suitcase. She remembered the door softly closing. She remembered lying on her side in bed, watching out the window as the sun sank over the Atlantic, and the next thing she knew, the sun had already returned, spilling across her bedspread and filling the room with light. Rubbing her eyes, she squinted at the wall clock opposite her bed. How was it this bright? It was 5:03 a.m. But then she remembered her mom's childhood stories about playing with her neighbors in the sun until nearly midnight, then waking up a few hours later to do it all again. It had something to do with the latitude of the island, those long northern summers. In the moleskin notebook next to her bed, she wrote,

1. Everybody talks about how it rains all the time in Ireland but nobody talks about how when the sun does shine, it shines all day and night
2. And when the sun goes down it looks like the ocean's catching on fire
3. Granda hates me

Outside, the pasture glittered with dew. Through the open window, she could hear the creak and boom of the morning sea. It was all so beautiful, and yet she couldn't help but think about how the rest of that long bright day, all the long bright days of the summer, loomed ahead of her. How would she fill them? Her mom had suggested going for refreshing walks around the farm and down to the sea. *Constitutionals*, she called them. Or swimming down at Inch Beach, though never so far out as to reach the darker waters. Or trying to meet some of the kids from the village. Or helping Granda with any house or farm chores that he needed done. As if Granda actually wanted her around. As if *she* wanted to be around *him*.

She pulled the covers over her head and decided she might as well go back to sleep. But she couldn't: it was too bright, and she couldn't stop thinking about the way Granda had looked at her last night after she'd vomited her dinner up all over his floor. It was just like the way Bella Martin and her posse had sneered at Breda after they found out about the stolen PE shorts, like she was a disgusting bug that wasn't even worth the effort it would take to squish.

Sleep was not going to come. She threw off her blankets and got dressed.

In the kitchen, Jake looked up sleepily from his little nest of old towels next to the radiator as Breda grabbed a couple pieces of sliced bread and slathered them with butter and elderberry jam.

As she took a bite, he lifted his head and twitched his ears, and when she peeled off a piece of crust and tossed it to him, he hopped out of his nest and caught it in his jaws. Breda laughed and petted him on the silky bridge of his snout. Folding a piece of bread into her own mouth, she stepped into her wellies and lifted her jacket off the peg next to the holy water font and opened the front door. Jake darted out behind her, leaping around her heels for more bread. Breda tossed him another crust and he weaved joyfully between her legs. She smiled and headed down the driveway. At least she'd made one friend in this house.

The cows chewed their grass and watched her as she marched down the driveway with Jake following at her heels. Together, girl and dog crossed the empty road to the wild other side. The beach grass was dry and tickly and came up to Breda's waist, skimming along the elbows of her nylon jacket. The ground was a muddy suck, and Jake hesitated at the edge until she lifted him into her arms, covering herself in paw prints in the process. It was a fight to get through the sharp, waving grass, but soon they broke through and were standing on an empty strand. The ground beneath Breda's boots was soft and gray, more like clay than sand. There were no boats, no ships, no people. Just Breda and Jake and a circle of screaming gulls in the sky above them, the glistening remains of a few washed-up jellyfish at their feet, and the water that went on and on until America.

As Jake explored the water's edge, nose snuffling along the sand, Breda stood looking out across the early morning water. It was easy to get lost in the overwhelming distance of that sun-dazzled seascape. It cleaned out her thoughts, cooled her hot, anxious brain. Sometimes it was like her feelings were just too big to contain, too scary to explore. *It's called puberty, babe*, her mother said. *Every one of us goes through it. Every one of us has to spend time as a knobbly little caterpillar before she can become a butterfly.* But Breda didn't feel like a butterfly in training. She felt like a cyclone; her moods jumping around, angry and tearful one minute and giggly the next, frightened for no reason, devastated and then thrilled by the smallest things. And then there was her body: her boobs growing heavier, her leg hair growing darker, and the pimples, the pimples! Not just on her face, but on her back sometimes, too, which she hadn't even known was a thing. She felt, more and more, like an actual monster. No wonder she had no friends. No wonder her mom had chosen the salon and their "financial future" over spending time with her. No wonder her dad had never bothered to come looking for her, or why she was stuck here for the summer with a cranky old farmer who knew nothing about her and didn't care to learn. Breda felt tears stinging her eyes—because, oh, that was another thing. She cried all the time now. She couldn't help it. If this was what growing up felt like, she'd rather be a caterpillar forever.

She dropped to her knees and scooped some of the ocean into her palm, tasting it before it dripped through her fingers. And as the salt dried on her lips, a strange thing happened: suddenly, for the flash of a second, she understood what it had been like to be her mother thirteen years ago, standing in this very place and looking out over the water with a hand on her growing belly, imagining life on the other side. Feeling the same kinds of swirling fears, the same uncontrollable emotions. Wanting so badly to leave this place. And wanting, just as badly, to stay.

The ocean is warmer than I expected, she wrote in her notebook.
And it tastes a little like olives.

II.

BREDA SPENT THE REST OF THAT FIRST full day in Dingle puttering around, watching the cows, exploring the sheds and hills and soft muddy pathways of Granda's farm. When evening came, still bright, Granda made a dinner of lamb chops and mashed potatoes, which was one of her favorite meals. Given the disaster of the previous night, she wondered if he had asked her mom what she liked to eat, or whether this was just a coincidence. Whatever the case, she ate everything on her plate, nibbling the lamb meat down to its hard white bones. Granda sat across from her with his own dinner, not smiling, exactly, but somehow managing to look pleased just the same at her newfound appetite.

Afterward, Breda went to her bedroom for a long, cool

shower. By the time she emerged from her bedroom, clean and dressed, and gone back down to the sitting room, Noeleen had arrived. The older woman was relaxing on the couch reading the *Kerryman*. Her face was painted with bright makeup and her hair was freshly washed, curled, and colored (blond highlights to smudge out the gray; it didn't look terrible, but Breda knew that her mom would have recommended a more natural-looking lowlight to blend with Noeleen's soft features). She wore a pair of white jeans with sparkly sandals and a matching blue sparkly top that showed off her thick freckled arms.

"Wow," Breda said, hanging by the doorway. "You look really nice."

"I s'pose I brush up alright." Noeleen touched her hair into place. "We're headed to the pub tonight. It's Davey's night to perform."

"He plays music, right?" Breda took a long swig from her water bottle. "Or sings or something?"

"Child, don't your mother tell you anything?"

Breda flinched. Where did he learn to move so quietly over those creaky old floorboards? Granda was standing right behind her, hands in his pockets, his face raw from shaving, his hair wet and combed. He wore pressed jeans, black shoes, and a short sleeve button-down shirt with blue checks all over it. He smelled like soap and aftershave. "I'm a seanchaí."

"A—what?"

"A seanchaí." He repeated the Irish word. *Shawn-a-key.* "A traditional storyteller. Tis a hobby of mine."

"Ah, Davey," said Noeleen, "tis more than a hobby. You're being modest." She smiled at him fondly, then turned to Breda. "Your granda is quite famous in these parts, as a matter of fact."

"Ach, sure." He shoved his hands in his pockets and looked out the window at the grazing cows.

"Back in the ancient times, the seanchaí held a position of esteem second only to kings and queens," Noeleen told Breda. "The clan leaders had the power, but the seanchaí had the memory. They were the brains of the island, holding the memories and passing down our stories before the monks arrived and taught us how to write."

"Get yourself tidied up," Granda said, still looking out the window. "I can't stand being late."

"What your granda *means* to say," Noeleen added with a wink, "is he would love it if you would join us."

12.

AS SOON AS THEY ARRIVED AT AN BRADÁN, a little stone pub at the edge of the village bustling with both locals and tourists, Granda peeled himself away from Noeleen and Breda, greeting and actually *laughing* with the other old men who were standing around holding their pints of beer and black instrument cases.

"The lads here," Noeleen explained, linking her arm in Breda's and walking her over to the group, "have been your granda's friends for decades now. JohnJoe plays the fiddle, and Jackie, in the red jumper, he's on guitar. Luke there will play the whistle and the squeeze-box." Breda gave them all a little wave, and they each nodded pleasantly back at her like they'd known her all their lives.

After she was finished making introductions, Noeleen led Breda over to a low table near the front of the room and went off to order them some drinks. She returned a few minutes later, handing Breda a bottle of Cidona and a glass with ice.

"So," Breda asked, pouring her cider, "if the seanchaí doesn't play an instrument or sing, then what does he actually *do*?"

"Exactly what the name implies—he tells stories." Noeleen settled into her seat, smiled at Breda, and squeezed her knee. She was happy and proud, Breda could tell, to be here with Granda. "You'll see."

Granda and his friends began by gathering in a circle and tuning their instruments. JohnJoe, Luke, and Jackie started off with a few trad tunes, just melodies without lyrics, while Granda sat on his stool with his hands resting on his knees, nodding his head and tapping his foot to the music. Then JohnJoe sang a few songs accompanied by Luke on the tin whistle—"The Boys of Barr Na Sráide" and "Nancy Spain," songs Breda knew from car rides with Nuala and from Christmas and Saint Patrick's Day parties at the Heritage Center. Her mom never listened to Irish music; she said that it made her sad. It only occurred to Breda now that maybe it made her sad not because it made her homesick but because it reminded her of Granda. After a few more tunes, the applause died down, and Granda cleared his throat to take the floor.

"As everyone knows," he began, speaking in a low, hushed voice, "banshees are tall, gaunt women spirits with long gray hair."

He leaned forward on his stool, resting his forearms on his knees, and the pub became as still as a nighttime cemetery. Tourists stopped scrolling through the pictures they'd taken earlier that day to give him their full attention, and even the barman, a young guy in an Adidas T-shirt with gelled black hair, crossed his arms and leaned against the till, listening.

"For thousands of years," Granda continued, "the banshee has been the most misunderstood of all of our spirit beings. She is to be feared—but she is not to be despised. She does not *kill*, as some mistakenly believe. She is only the *harbinger* of death. Her purpose is to warn Irish families that death is coming, so they can get their souls in order. Which means that she, more than any of the other spirits, is on the side of *us*—of human beings.

"And how does she warn us that death is lurking near? Why, by her distinctive, bone-chilling wail, of course. A man might be in bed, sleeping, and be awoken by a sound that at first he thinks to be the wind blowing off the sea. But then she calls to him again, and he recognizes it at once, for tis a sound not heard in nature, and it freezes the blood. Now he knows the banshee has come and suffering is soon to follow.

"During famine times, when death was everywhere, killing off our people by the millions, tis said that the banshee's call across the bogs and quiet hills of western Ireland was so loud and ceaseless that those who emigrated to America flocked to the big cities—New York, Chicago, Boston—not for work, as you might imagine, but in hopes that the noise of the city would drown out their memories of that lonely, terrible sound."

At that, Granda leaned back, lifted his face to the ceiling, and howled. Most of the tourists in the pub gasped; a flush-cheeked woman in an Aran sweater and pink visor actually shrieked. Breda sat stunned. She could not believe this desperate sound, which sent goose bumps shooting up her arms, could have come from such a cold and serious man.

"Though tis less common," Granda went on once the crowd had again quieted, "there have been times that the banshee has allowed herself to be seen. A man here in Dingle, farmer in Ventry—he saw her once, leaning against one of his hedgerows, holding one of his new lambs mewling in her arms. The next morning his whole flock was stone dead, wiped out from the braxy. The poor farmer's whole livelihood was lost, and his family became destitute.

"Another man I know—man from down in Cahersiveen—saw the banshee early one morning, standing square in the middle of his garden, a stony expression on her face. As the sun rose behind her, the banshee stared at him with cold limestone eyes and began slowly combing her long gray hair. Later that week, while his wife was standing before her mirror preparing for mass, she fell to the floor, dead in an instant. Stroke, I believe it was." He looked around at the crowd, his eyes gleaming, as if it gave him great pleasure to know how easily he could hold them all in his sway. "Every one of us will hear the wail of the banshee, you see, and so you may as well learn to recognize it. It could be ten years from now, or twenty. Or it could be this very night as you lie cozy in your hotel room, believing yourself to be safe. Not a one of us is immune from her nighttime voice— she will come calling for us all, someday."

At this, Breda felt a sudden bristling inside herself—a distinct and creeping feeling that someone was watching her. She turned her head swiftly, half terrified of what kind of long-haired woman spirit might be standing in the pub's shadows. So it was with some relief that she realized it was no spirit staring her down, but an actual person. The pub's cook. He was dressed in chef's whites, with blondish hair, a light beard, and pale, searching eyes. Only his face was visible, framed by the serving hatch that looked out from the kitchen into the main room of the pub. As soon as he realized that she'd seen him, though, he disappeared from the window so fast that it was easy for Breda to think she'd just imagined the whole thing.

The night went on like this—with music and songs, and Granda's tales in between. He told the story of a man who was in love with his sailboat. Of four young children who were turned into swans by their jealous stepmother, the queen. Of a fairy, disguised as a black dog, who tried to sneak into a cottage and eat a family's firstborn baby son. Whenever he spoke, the audience hung on his every word, and Breda could see why Noeleen had been so proud to walk into An Bradán at his side. She found herself so swept away by the music and stories that she almost forgot about the cook and his stare. But then, as the night was coming to an end and the musicians warmed up for their last song, she looked up to find that he was standing right next to her.

"Hiya," he said, nodding at Noeleen as he reached across Breda to grab her empty glass and add it to the wobbly stack he had gathered from the other tables. "The lads sounded good tonight."

"Hello, Sully." Noeleen glanced up at him but didn't smile. Her voice was cool, almost rude. It surprised Breda. Noeleen was so warm and friendly, but the way she was speaking to the cook sounded more like, well, Granda. "I didn't know you worked here now."

"Just picking up a few shifts here and there." He shot her a lopsided grin. "Helping out for tourist season."

"Ah." Noeleen took her phone from her purse and began tapping at it. Her body language was loud and clear: *leave us alone*. Sully, whoever he was, seemed to get the hint. But before he walked away, he glanced over at Breda again, as if he half expected her to ask him to pull up a stool and join them. When she didn't, he slouched away toward the kitchen with his empty glasses. Noeleen put her phone down and sighed.

"Who was *that*?" Breda asked.

"No one but Mícheál Sullivan. Went to school with your mother. And he's got *some* amount of nerve coming over here."

"What do you mean? Why?"

"Oh"—she waved—"he's just a pure amadán. He don't much care for a day's work. Always running around with one woman or another. And you wouldn't see him at Sunday mass if Jesus Christ himself sent a personal invitation." She glared across the pub at Mícheál Sullivan's retreating figure, then looked over at Granda, who was helping JohnJoe make some adjustment to his fiddle strings. "Listen, love: let's not mention to Davey that he came over talking to us. Is that alright? We're having such a lovely night, and I don't want anything to spoil it."

Breda shrugged. She thought about asking more, but she knew what she was dealing with: her family believed in leaving mysteries intact and things unsaid. "Okay."

"Now." Noeleen smiled, reaching across the table to squeeze Breda's hand. "Tell me what you thought of our seanchaí."

Breda smiled back. "I thought he was wonderful."

And she meant it. After Noeleen dropped them off and Breda had changed into her pajamas and crawled into bed, she found that she couldn't sleep. The night had been so unexpected and strange. It was as if the moment Granda stepped into his role as seanchaí, the tightly curled fist of who he was slowly opened up. His impatience became wisdom; his crankiness became knowledge of secret, ancient ways.

Breda thought back to one of the few bright spots of seventh grade, the Halloween story contest Mr. Ramirez had assigned to her class. Poor Mr. Ramirez; he was one of those teachers who tried so hard even though none of his students took him very seriously. Even after he'd announced the grand prize for the best story—a fifty-dollar Chili's gift card—no one but Breda seemed to care about the assignment. Some kids wrote about jack-o'-lanterns or witches with broomsticks and black pointy hats—baby stuff, uninspired. Others hastily typed up their stories in the computer lab before school on the morning the assignment was due, and a few even plagiarized straight from the internet. But Breda spent a whole week on her story, working late into the night because her mom was too busy to enforce a bedtime. While the autumn wind howled outside and rain lashed against the cheap old windows of their rented house, she composed a story about a herd of zombie moose, roaming the snowy Alaskan wilderness, trampling oil-drilling sites, eating people's pets, and goring anyone who tried to cause injury to their endangered habitat with their huge zombie antlers. She had no idea where the story had come from—she had never been to Alaska and knew nothing about moose, or oil drilling. But the story had poured out of her all the same, from beginning to end, as if it had been sitting in her brain all along, patiently waiting for her to discover it. She'd entitled her masterpiece "Moose on the Loose" (admitting to her mom, afterward, that the title was the weakest part), and much to her shock, it won the grand prize. A few weeks after Halloween, her mom had closed the salon early and the two of them got dressed up and went out for a feast of ribs and quesadillas. When the check arrived, Breda threw down her gift card, feeling like a celebrity, while her mom took pictures. She could get used to this, she remembered thinking: this feeling of being good at something.

1. The banshee's eyes are the color of limestone
2. Real fairies are nothing like Tinker Bell; they are

bloodthirsty shape-shifters who disguise themselves as dogs, snakes, or old men
3. Amadán is Irish for idiot
4. Did I inherit my storytelling skills from Granda?

She closed her notebook and put it back on her nightstand. But just as she was nestling into her covers for a contented, restful sleep, that was when the screaming began.

13.

GRANDA WAS LYING RIGID ON HIS BACK, HIS gnarled fingers clinging to his quilt, his eyes squeezed shut. "Please," he was screaming, over and over again. "Please please please." The sound of it was terrible, just as her mother had warned. It was the scream of a terrified child, coming from the mouth of an old man who normally seemed so tough and strong. He'd be furious if he knew Breda was standing in his bedroom, seeing him this way. She wanted nothing more than to go back to her own bed and press her hands against her ears until it was over, but she knew what she had to do: if she didn't wake him up, he would just keep screaming.

She approached his bed. The moonlight coming through the gauzy white curtains made his skin look pale and waxy.

"Please," he shouted. "Please, no!"

"Granda," she whispered, gently touching his shoulder.

"No!"

"Granda," she repeated, a little louder this time. She put her hand on his shoulder again, her fingers digging into the pack of muscle beneath his yellow striped pajama shirt. "Granda, wake up. You're dreaming."

"Please, sister—"

"Granda!" she shouted, and shook his arm, hard.

As he jerked away from her touch, his eyes flew open, flashing blue in the moonlight, wild with terror.

"Who—"

"Granda. You were having a bad dream."

He sat up and covered his face with his hands, which were trembling so hard she wanted to take them into her own to still them.

"It's okay," she said gently, perching herself at the edge of his bed. "It's over now."

He looked at her, breathing deeply. Lying there in his yellow striped pajamas, his silver hair wild from sleep and sweat, he looked so old that it felt to her that the way he acted during the day was a disguise, that this was who he really was: just a very fragile elderly man, haunted by things that she would never understand.

"Christ," he said, slumping down against his headboard.

"What were you dreaming about, Granda?" she asked him softly. "What did you see?"

"Not a thing worth talking about. Just a silly dream was all it was." He tried to smile at her, but without his dentures, his mouth looked small and puckered. "Sorry for frightening you like that, Breda. You can go on back to bed now."

"But—"

"Go on, child. I'm grand."

Breda stood up. "Okay, but can I get you some tea or something?"

"I'm grand," he repeated woodenly. "I'm perfectly grand now."

"Well, alright." She reached across the covers and held her hand over his for a moment. It was still trembling. "Good night, Granda."

"Good night, love."

It was only when she crawled back to her own bed, her heart still pounding, that she realized: he had never called her *love* before.

14.

THE NEXT MORNING, GRANDA JOINED
Breda for an early breakfast, placidly chewing his toast
as if nothing strange had happened the night before. She tried
not to stare at him as she wondered just what it was in his quiet
farmer's life that tortured him in the night. Was it the death of
his wife when Breda's mom was still just a toddler? Was it the
loss of his only child to the call of America? Or was it something else, something even darker and deeper, something he'd
pressed so far down in his mind it chose to punish him in his
dreams? Of course she couldn't ask him any of this. She wanted
to, but she didn't dare.

When they finished eating, they washed their breakfast
dishes together in silence, side by side at the kitchen sink.

Drying her hands on the faded red dish towel, Breda was just about to retreat back to her bedroom to grab her notebook and figure out how she was going to pass the rest of the day when Granda walked over to the front door and held it open.

"C'mere, child," he said as Jake bolted past him and out into the driveway. "I've something to show you."

"What is it?"

"In my day, children didn't ask questions. They simply obeyed their elders."

Breda sighed, slipped on her wellies, and followed him out the door and across the asphalt as he disappeared into the main shed behind the house. Inside the big low building, the air was damp, smelling of oil and cut wood, and although it was cluttered, there seemed to be a designated place for everything. In this way it reminded her a little of her mom's salon. But instead of a neat closet full of hair color tubes arranged from brightest blond to deepest black, as well as the pinks and blues of her mom's more adventurous clients, here there were shelves lined with old biscuit tins, labeled with masking tape—WORK GLOVES, TWIST DRILLS, LOCK NUTS, WASHERS, CASTRATION BANDS, and more. There were neatly stacked cans of paint, barrels filled with old bottles and crushed cans, a clothesline draped with several pairs of rubber coveralls, a dust-furred radio blasting pop music.

"I didn't think you were an Ariana Grande type of guy, Granda," Breda said.

"Who?"

She nodded toward the radio.

"Ah." He stuffed a chaw of tobacco into his lower lip. "Loud music scares the rats away. So. What'd you make of the session last night?"

"It was really cool," she said. "You guys were great, Granda."

"Twas a good old session, so it was." He leaned out the doorway and spat a brown stream of saliva into the grass. Then he turned on his heel and disappeared into the clutter. A few moments later he remerged, wheeling a shiny blue mountain bike.

"Tis a fair bit old," he said, flicking down the kickstand with the toe of his boot. "Twas your mother's, but I fitted it with new tires and brakes when she told me you were coming to stay."

Breda went over to the bike. She could feel his eyes on her as she ran her hand along the smooth leather seat.

"Wow, Granda," she said. "It's really nice."

"Ach, sure." He squinted up at the rafters of the shed, where a small brown bird was busily adding twigs to her nest. "Twill give you something to do while you're here this summer. I s'posed I ought to just give it to you, rather than leave it lying around for you to steal."

Breda could feel the smile curdling on her face. She let go of the handles as fast as if they were dipped in lava.

"Ah, that was a joke now." Granda reached out and caught the bike before it clattered to the floor. "I didn't mean no harm by it."

She nodded but didn't say anything. She knew that if she tried to speak, she would start to cry. And anyway, she could never explain to Granda that it was never even about the stuff—she had never really wanted any of it. It was just that she had tried other things. She had tried keeping her room immaculate and she had tried getting perfect grades. She had even tried making dinner a few times—mushy spaghetti, overcooked chicken— but even then, her mom, overwhelmed with the salon's opening months, had only noticed when she'd pointed it out. *Look at me, Mom. Look at what I did. Look at how good I am.* But with the stealing? She suddenly had her mom's full and undivided attention without having to ask for it. Of course Granda would never understand that, let alone forgive it, because stealing was a sin, and you can't commit a sin just to make yourself stop feeling invisible.

"Erm." He coughed for a moment, then cleared his throat. "Anyhow. Sorry there about that ruckus last night."

Breda shrugged, running her hand along the glossy blue surface of the bike frame.

"My boyhood was rough." He glared at the concrete shed floor. "Sometimes it comes back to me."

"Oh." She glanced back up at him in surprise. In the short time she'd been in Ballyglass, this was the most personal he'd ever gotten with her. "I—I'm sorry, Granda."

"What do you have to be sorry about, child? Sure it happened, and now tis over. There's no use boiling cabbage twice." He bared his teeth to spit some more tobacco juice out the doorway, then dragged the bike out into the driveway while Breda followed behind. "Now. Go ahead and try her out so."

Breda adjusted the seat, climbed aboard, and rode a few figure eights around the driveway. It was a good bike, she could see that already. Better than the one she had back home, the one her mom had bought on Facebook Marketplace with the rust spots blooming over the crossbar. He handed her a shiny new helmet, blue to match the bike, and she put it on, adjusting the strap beneath her chin.

"You can take it anywhere you like," Granda said, watching her as he leaned against the shed. "Tisn't America and I ain't one of them American grandparents who hovers and spoils and watches over you every moment of the day. I've a farm to manage."

Breda stifled the urge to roll her eyes. Granda acted like freedom was something new for her: he had no clue that she'd spent all of seventh grade practically raising herself.

"If you go that way," Granda said now, pointing to the narrow road that hugged the sea, "you're on the road to Dingle town, and eventually, the very western edge of Ireland. There's good beaches down that way, but there are also loads of tourists who haven't a clue how to drive these roads. You must keep your wits about you if you ride on the Dingle road. I've nearly been killed myself more than once by a carload of Yanks drifting into my lane.

"In the other direction is the road to the village. Ain't much to do there. You can get an ice cream at the petrol station, send a postcard to your mother if you like. Light a candle in the church. The village is safe, so you may go nearly anywhere within its borders that you please. Like I said, Ballyglass ain't like America. All that crime and violence, I never understood the appeal, myself."

Breda gripped the rubber handlebars as she half listened. She was itching to get moving, to feel the salt breeze whip her hair and the Irish sun freckle her face.

"One more thing. As I said, you may go *nearly* anywhere you like in the village. There is one exception. There are two pubs in Ballyglass, yeah? One is An Bradán, where we played last night. They do a lovely toasted sandwich; you're welcome there anytime. But you may not, under any circumstances, darken the door of the other place. Understand me? Not ever."

"Why not?"

"What did I just say about children simply *obeying* without asking questions?" He folded his arms over his chest and thought for a moment. "But I s'pose I should warn you, giving your criminal tendencies. The Faheys who run the place are a rough old crowd. Not a shred of ethics in the lot of them. Your mother sent you here so that I could see to your moral education. T'would be an awful thing indeed if you fell in with the likes of them. Now. Those clear skies mightn't last more than an hour or two. Go on with you, while you've still got the weather."

Breda flicked up the kickstand and pushed off with one foot. The driveway sloped downward, and she was already flying. Granda had said that he wouldn't be keeping an eye on her, and yet when she reached the road and looked back toward the house, there he was, still standing there. She turned west toward the beaches, feeling his pale eyes boring into her back until long after she'd disappeared from view.

15.

THAT FIRST WEEK OF RIDING, IT TOOK
everything Breda had in her skinny arms and legs to
coax her bike up even some of the milder hills. She was used
to the flat, gridded streets of Chicago, not twisting mountain
roads with hairpin turns and steep inclines. But she pushed on,
sweat pouring down her face despite the stiff wind blowing
off the sea, and when she reached the crest of her biggest hill
one fine morning, she received her reward. Hundreds of yards
below was a long strand rolling into the surf, with little trailers
parked up on the sand and green rocky cliffs tumbling into the
water. She didn't even need a map to recognize it: the world-
famous Inch Beach. Breda pushed off from the top of the hill,

her stomach dropping like a tossed coin, her tires nearly float-ing free of the road. When she reached the beach, she came upon a little shack at the edge of the water. She wheeled her bike inside the sandy-floored building—even if Granda said there was no crime here, she still wasn't about to leave it unlocked and unattended; having been one herself, she knew there were thieves everywhere—and took a minute for her eyes to adjust to the dim coolness.

"Morning," the woman behind the counter said. "What will you have?"

"Um." Breda scanned the menu on a chalkboard next to the television—fish and chips, chicken goujons, toasted ham and cheese, vegetable soup and brown bread. Her stomach growled. She could hear the hiss of hot oil back in the kitchen as a wire basket of fries was dipped into it. But this was a tourist beach, with tourist prices. Her shampoo tips and the extra money her mom had given her was meant to last the summer, and if she ran out, she'd have to ask Granda for more. That was not something she wanted to do. "I'll just have a glass of water with blackcurrant," she said. "And a bag of Taytos, please."

The woman nodded, pulled the bag of chips from their clip above the till, and poured Breda a glass of water mixed with a few splashes of purple sweetener.

"One euro eighty."

Breda counted out the coins slowly—she was still learning the currency—and pushed them across the counter. When she looked up, the woman at the till was staring at her.

"You look fierce familiar," she said, sweeping the change into her palm. "You're not a Sullivan, are you?"

Breda shook her head.

"Funny." She counted out the change and handed it over with a suspicious squint. "You look *just* like a Sullivan. You've got the eyes."

Sullivan. As in Mícheál Sullivan, the man who'd been staring at her with that strange, probing look the night of Granda's session? With those eyes that were just like her own, apparently? She wondered again why Noeleen had behaved so strangely toward the cook that night. And why did she make Breda promise not to tell Granda they'd spoken? Maybe, she thought, gathering up her coins, it didn't mean anything. Sullivan was as common a name in Ireland as Smith was in the US. And millions of people had blue eyes. And if Granda didn't like the guy, so what? Granda didn't like *anyone*.

And yet, as Breda wheeled her bike back outside, past a crowd of backpackers who carried with them the smell of sweat and sunscreen, she couldn't ignore the question flickering in her heart, the question she'd been quietly carrying all her life, that had become louder ever since that day at Sophie Taylor's birthday party: *Is your dad from Ireland, too?*

All at once, the answer suddenly felt near enough to touch.

16.

WITH A NEW BIKE AND PLENTY OF NEW things to think about while riding it, the days began to pass swiftly. In the mornings, if Breda woke early enough, she could ride for hours without encountering a single other human being. Noeleen had given her a paper map of the Dingle Peninsula, and Breda's goal for the summer was to ride from Granda's farm all the way out to Dún Chaoin, the green tendril of land that marked the western edge of Europe and the last stop before America. These solitary mornings were her favorite time of day, filled with gray crashing water, silent green cliffs, and jackdaws and gannets wheeling against the cloud-streaked sky like black and white chess pieces. The cool air was filled with the clean scent of grass and turf smoke. Even the less pleasing smells—the stink of decaying crab washed up by the shore, or the slurry from the dairy farms, so strong it felt oily in her nostrils—even that, on these mornings, Breda was growing to love.

There were sleepy little villages along her riding route that were so small she could coast through them from beginning to end without pressing her pedals. There were the mossy stone remains of Minard Castle, five hundred years old according to its plaque. All over the peninsula were other ruins—ring forts and strange cairns many hundreds of years older than even that. And there were all sorts of animals she'd never seen before. One day, she was nearly scared off her bike by a big brown-and-white bird—a corncrake, Noeleen explained to her later that evening over fresh bacon and boiled cabbage—a low-flying, clumsy creature that had burst soundlessly from a stand of furze and nearly collided with the spokes of her wheels. Another perfect afternoon, she saw, in the span of a single hour, the red blur of a fox streaking up a rocky hill and the smooth wet back of a dolphin breaching in Castlemaine Harbour. There were lounging sea otters and loping blue hare, frogs and toads hopping in the brush and countless seabirds calling out from the sky.

As each day passed, Breda loved Dingle more and more. But Granda, on the other hand, remained as distant and remote to her as the silhouettes of the Blasket Islands far out on the water. He never spoke to her again of his terrible dreams, and the nights, for now, remained quiet. It seemed to Breda that even if she stayed at the farm for a hundred summers, she could never really know him; that the closest she could ever get was to learn to know the land. So that's what she did, morning after morning, all through the long days of June.

Dingle Observations!!

The hump of An Blascaod Mór can turn black and purple and sometimes even pink, depending on the time of day and the way the light is hitting.

A few miles from here there is a rock with fossilized salamander footprints that are 385 million years old (!!!)

Some beaches out here are dotted with huge, smooth boulders, tossed onto land by the sea. Granda says these beaches are called storm strands.

The birds that fly so high above water that they look like bats or drones are called kestrels.

Noeleen says that the ancient people in this place used sphagnum moss for toilet paper. 😊

17.
JULY

I F IT HADN'T BEEN FOR DINGLE'S STRANGE coastal weather, where a glorious sunny day could morph quickly into a lashing downpour, perhaps July would have unspooled as quietly as June had, filled with bike rides and the occasional trip to An Bradán to see Granda perform; searching for but never again seeing the strange Mícheál Sullivan, the man who—she could barely allow herself to think it—might actually be her dad. But on that particular afternoon in early July, a warm if overcast day, one minute she was riding contentedly down the main road of Ballyglass, and the next, the skies blackened and a cold rain came blowing off the sea and sheeting down, soaking her clean through in seconds. So Breda did what anyone would do: she propped her bike against the nearest shop wall and ducked through its open doorway. Afterward, she would tell herself that it wasn't her fault, in the same way that stealing felt less wrong when she didn't plan doing it ahead of time, when stolen objects just seemed to drift into her hands, her pockets, her backpack.

Inside, a girl, just a few years older than Breda, was sitting behind a large desk made of polished wood. She had a pile of auburn hair pulled into a bun at the top of her head with a bright yellow scrunchie. She was drinking a bottle of 7Up while tapping and swiping with great concentration at her phone. She didn't even look up when Breda walked in, which gave Breda a moment to take in her surroundings. The place was old and a bit musty, but clearly well loved. The carpets were dark red, patterned with diamonds. There was a small sitting area with two sun-bleached red velvet chairs and a little glass round table between them, where a bowl of dusty plastic flowers were arranged. Behind the chairs was a fireplace, and there, in carved wooden letters hanging above the mantel:

Fáilte go Ó Fathaigh
Welcome to Fahey's

Just as Breda was realizing she was standing in the one place on this island she was strictly forbidden to be, and gathering her breath to brave it back through the rain and down to An Bradán instead, the girl behind the counter looked up from her phone.

"Lashing rain," she said, nodding out toward the window.

"I got caught in it on my bike," Breda answered. "I'll be on my way as soon as it lets up."

"You're grand sure." The girl shrugged. "Stay as long as you like."

Breda smiled uneasily. "Thanks."

"So you're a Yank," the girl observed, picking at one of her long nails. "Boston? New York?"

"Chicago."

"Lovely. The Windy City. I've always wanted to go. You here on holidays?"

"No, I—" Breda stopped. She was about to explain how she was staying with her granda for the summer on his farm outside the village, but then this girl would probably ask who her granda was, and it occurred to her that if he had such a problem with the Faheys, then maybe the Faheys had just as big a problem with him. "Yeah. On holidays."

The girl squinted past Breda and looked through the doorway. For a moment, the empty street lit up, and a crack of thunder reverberated through the dusty room.

"Well, I was just about to take my lunch, and you may as well join me. It don't look like twill let up anytime soon."

Next to the hotel reception desk was another doorway, and through it Breda could hear television commentary about a hurling match, the clinking of glasses and plates, murmured conversations and the occasional spike of laughter. Fahey's Pub. So the hotel and the pub were connected, a common arrangement in Ireland, where many families who owned pubs often lived upstairs, or rented out the adjoining rooms for extra income. Ballyglass was a tiny place. If she went through this doorway with this girl, there was a good chance Granda would find out about it.

"I actually just ate," Breda said. "But thank you."

"Ah, look at the size of you. You haven't a pick of weight on those bones. You could use another feed, I'd say."

"But I didn't bring my money."

"Not a bother. My dad owns the place. I don't pay for my meals and neither do my friends. I'm Nellie, by the way. What'd you say your name was?"

"Um—I didn't, but it's Breda."

"Breda. Come on, then." She grabbed a little placard that said BACK IN THIRTY MINUTES and placed it in the middle of the reception desk. Before Breda could protest further, Nellie led her toward the pub door, just as another crash of thunder sent the overhead lights blinking in their sockets.

18.

NELLIE FAHEY WAS FOURTEEN, BREDA learned, the only girl in a family of five kids—two younger boys, two older, and *me, smack in the middle of all that madness.*

"Hey, Dad," she called to the man behind the counter as they walked into the pub. His hair was red, fading to silver around the temples, and he had deep smile lines around his eyes. He wore a Manchester United jersey and a pair of yellow tracksuit pants. "This is Breda."

"Hiya," the man said, and returned his attention to the hurling match on TV. Nellie pointed out a table surrounded by low stools, and told Breda to have a seat. Then she disappeared into the kitchen, leaving Breda to sit there, looking out the window at the pouring rain and hoping none of the local men at the counter recognized her as Davey Moriarity's granddaughter. Soon enough, Nellie came back through the swinging kitchen door, carrying a plate in each hand.

"Best shepherd's pie in The Kingdom," Nellie promised, setting the plate in front of her. It was a flaky butter pastry with crimped fork marks around the edges and three neat slashes in the middle where a delicious meaty steam escaped.

"What's The Kingdom?"

"An Ríocht. The Kingdom. That's what we call Kerry, because it's Ireland's greatest county. In my totally unbiased opinion, of course." Nellie sat down on the stool across from Breda and picked up her cutlery. "So. Where you staying? Dingle town?"

"No, but I'm, um, staying out on the road that way." Breda blew on a forkful of potatoes, carrots, and mince.

"Oh, grand. There's some good B and Bs out that way. Not as good as ours, of course. Which one?"

"*Wow.*" Breda swallowed, the rich stew warming her whole belly. "This really *is* the best shepherd's pie I've ever had."

"Family recipe." Nellie smiled proudly, and Breda took the opportunity to quickly change the subject.

"So, what's there to do around here?"

"Well, my dad's got me working all the time," said Nellie,

"so I'm always missing the craic. But the beach is a grand time in the summers. And a shot of us like to play football down at the pitch on Friday evenings. You've never played Gaelic football, I s'pose. You probably don't even know what it is."

Breda thought of all those early mornings down at Galvin's, the Irish pub in their Chicago neighborhood, when she and her mom would don their green-and-yellow jerseys and go for a big breakfast of sausages and rashers, black pudding and fried eggs, to cheer on County Kerry in the all-Ireland. Kerry football was the piece of home her mom had carried with her most strongly in her nearly thirteen years in the US. In Kerry, Breda knew, Gaelic football was more than a game; it was identity; it was culture; it was an obsession.

"I know what Gaelic football is," she said.

Nellie raised a skeptical eyebrow. "You ever played, so?"

"Not really."

Which wasn't exactly true. She'd done a couple cúl camps in summers past, when her mom needed her out of the house all day so she could work. There, Breda had learned the basics of the game, which was sort of like soccer and sort of like rugby and sort of like American football but also completely different from all three. She'd learned the various offensive and defensive principles, how to fist pass and dribble the ball, how to punt it over the crossbar for a point and kick it into the net for three.

She hadn't been the best player on the field, but, to her great surprise, she also hadn't been the worst.

"Why don't you come play with us this Friday? We need more girls. Tis a bit of craic anyway."

"I'm not very good."

"You're tall. And you've big hands and feet, which is useful." Breda felt her cheeks flame. Big hands and feet? Was this Nellie's version of a compliment? "The pitch is on the sea side of the road down to Castlemaine. You can't miss it. Half seven is when we start picking teams. You'll come, won't you?"

Breda put down her fork and looked across the table at Nellie. The girl was small in stature, with a spate of freckles across her cheekbones. She had a slight overbite, a delicate chin, and clear, bright eyes. Granda had warned that everyone in the Fahey family was a criminal, but it was hard to see anything sneaky about Nellie. In fact, she had just been nicer to Breda than any of her classmates back in Chicago had ever been. Year after year, during Girl Scouts or ballet class or summer camp, Breda had watched pairs of girls buzz over to one another, link arms, and then, for the rest of the school year or the season, neither girl ever had to be alone again. Breda had never been a half of one of those connections. Maybe this could be her chance?

Still, she felt a stab of guilt. As quiet and grumpy as Granda was, he was still her family, and she'd made a promise to him.

He already thought she was a thief; what would he think of her if he found out she'd disobeyed him to hang out with a criminal Fahey? Then again, even if he'd forbidden her to set foot in Fahey's Pub, he'd never said anything about hanging out with a Fahey *outside* of the pub, now had he? The chance of finally finding real friendship—even if it was just for the summer—was too enticing to turn down. Breda smiled across the table at Nellie.

"Sure," she said. "Count me in."

19.

THAT FRIDAY, WHILE THE EVENING SUN was still high overhead, Breda climbed onto her bicycle and rode west toward the town of Castlemaine, near the web of land between Dingle and the main island.

The football pitch was a rectangle of bright green grass at the edge of the water behind the village school. There were huge nets strung up behind the western goalpost, to prevent wayward footballs from splashing into the sea. When Breda arrived, there were already ten or eleven kids there, and the coach was warming them up with passing drills. Nellie's shock of auburn curls stood out brightly against the green, and Breda recognized her as soon as she leaned her bike against the stone fence that separated the field from the road. She took a deep breath, feeling a sudden stab of anxiety. All these kids—what if they didn't like her? What if they made fun of her accent or her big hands and feet? What if she was awful, and ruined the match for everyone? She was about to turn around and ride home, to the safety of the farm and Granda's silence and his evening television programs, but just then Nellie saw her, waved, and came jogging over. It was too late to leave.

"You made it, Yank!" She tossed the football to Breda, who caught it, hard, against her chest. "C'mon with me, I'll introduce you to the gang."

There were too many names for Breda to keep track of, but it was easy to tell who was a Fahey because they all had curly hair in varying shades of red. There were Nellie's two older brothers, Daniel and Seamus, and her cousins, Louise, Niall, and Elaine. Then there was a handful of other village kids, who looked at her with mild curiosity but otherwise didn't pay her much attention, which was a relief. Breda didn't mind that she was chosen last when teams were picked; she was used to it from gym class, and anyway, why would a bunch of Irish kids expect a Yank to know anything about football?

And maybe that was why, when they began their scrimmage, Breda surprised everyone, herself most of all, by not actually being terrible. She remembered the basics of football from cúl camp, and because she could perform them with limited skill when the Irish kids had expected her not to be able to perform them at all, she appeared better than she actually was. Plus, the time she'd already spent riding her bike all over the peninsula had made her body much stronger than it had ever felt before. Halfway through the scrimmage, Saoirse, a black-eyed wiry girl in a Liverpool top, dribbled the ball down the field and passed it to Breda, who was standing at a right angle near the goal line. The ball landed smoothly between her palms, and though she was close enough to try to kick it into the net—a goal, worth three points—she lost her nerve and punted it instead, as hard as she could. It shot over the bar, between the goalposts. She had scored her first point, ever, in any sport. Seamus, sixteen and thick as a grain silo, shouted at her for not trying for a goal. But even that felt good; it meant he had believed she'd been capable of it.

By the time the scrimmage ended, Breda was dripping with sweat and her muscles felt electric and vibrating, the way they did after a good bike ride. It was as if her body, which had been betraying her so often lately with pimples and unexpected periods and growing breasts and aching shins, was hers once more. It felt wonderful.

"Good match, Yank." Nellie slung her arm around Breda's damp shoulders and offered her a bottle of Lucozade from the cooler her older brother had brought along. "Next week, same place, same time?"

"Okay." Breda bit her lip, smiling.

"And next time, try for a goal, yeah?" Seamus squirted some water into his mouth, rolled it around in his cheeks, and spat it into the grass.

"I will."

That night, as she rode back to Granda's, she couldn't shake the smile from her face. She, Breda Moriarity, had found herself a group of friends. And the shocking thing was, it hadn't even been that hard. True, most of them were Faheys, which wasn't exactly ideal, but hey: what Granda didn't know couldn't hurt him. The nighttime sun was still high overhead, and the mountain-rimmed sea, the farms and hills looked both grand and familiar. They were places she had come to know—places she belonged. That night, for the first time, Dingle felt like home.

20.

SOMETIME LATER THAT SAME NIGHT, THE fine weather turned, and Breda awoke from a deep sleep with the rain pouring down outside her window. There was no thunder, no lightning, just a loud hissing that drummed hypnotically on the slate roof. She squinted up at the clock, glowing in the faint light of the Blessed Virgin Mary's fake candle. It was two in the morning. Outside, even in the darkness, she could see a patch of moon through the clouds, and the moon reflected the white foam tops of the sea, which thrashed angrily, nearly higher than the beach grass across the road. She lay there for a few moments, watching the sky, before cuddling back beneath her mother's worn covers. She was just slipping away when she heard a sudden, frightening sound. It was louder than the drumbeat of the rain. Someone was screaming.

Not again, thought Breda.

"Granda?" she called. There was no answer. She threw her covers off and stood there listening. Another scream rolled through the house, filled with pain and fear. But it didn't sound like it was coming from down the hall—it sounded like it came from outside, somewhere beyond in the wet, windy darkness of the vast farm. Breda shivered, remembering Granda's seanchaí story about the banshee and her warning wails, then tiptoed toward his bedroom. As soon as she got into the hall, though, she saw that his door was already wide open. She peered in. His blankets were in a pile at the end of the bed and the bed was empty. He was gone.

She ran down the hall now, her heart a pit of dread. In the kitchen, she flicked on the light, and saw that Jake's little nest of towels, too, was empty. Could Granda be hurt out in the pasture somewhere, or worse? Was it even a human scream that beckoned her into the night? Or was it the cry of the banshee? Whatever it was, Breda had to see for herself. There was no one else to do it for her. She grabbed her rain jacket off the peg next to the holy water, stuffed her bare feet into her wellies, and ran outside, the kitchen door banging shut behind her.

The screams were coming from up near the base of the hill. Breda fumbled her way across the driveway and reached the open door of the garage shed. Inside, a small light was on, and, without Ariana Grande to scare them away, Breda was sure she could hear the rustling and skittering of rats. She knew Granda kept two flashlights on a hook inside the doorway, and in the dim light she could see that one was missing. She grabbed the other, clicked it on, and stifled her own scream. With the wind gusting in from the open doorway, Granda's rubber coveralls, hung up with clothespins, waved and spun like a living being—like a banshee.

She stumbled out of the shed, slamming the door behind her. With a cone of light to lead her way, she picked through the mud, following the screams toward the big barn. Inside the huge sliding doorway, a lantern hung from a beam, and the first thing Breda saw as she walked through was Granda's shadow thrown against the back wall. He wasn't hurt or in distress, and her knees buckled with relief. He was standing in one of the stalls with the same cow that had been watching Breda with liquid brown eyes her first day in Ballyglass. The cow was shaking her head very slowly back and forth and lowing to herself over and over. Breda realized now that it had been the animal's screams that had awoken her.

"Is her baby coming?" Breda hung at the doorway, her voice small.

"The pins dropped not too long ago. Come over here; I'll show you."

In the light of the lantern, all of Granda's features were exaggerated, his wrinkles deep and craggy across his face. She stepped toward him, not wanting to get too close to the distressed creature, but he reached out, took her by the wrist, and placed her hand near the top of the cow's rear end.

"See these two little pin bones on either side of her tail? These are usually higher up, level with the top of the tail. But they're after dropping now, do you feel that?"

Breda nodded, her palm cupping the thin arch of bone beneath the animal's hide.

"That's the best way to know when a calf's ready to be born." He sat back on his haunches. "It should have happened by now. I can't reckon why it hasn't."

The cow lifted her heavy, blunt head, shuffled back and forth in her stall, and cried out again. It was a terrible sound, desperate and wild, more like the roar of a forest bear than the sounds made by a docile creature, raised for its milk and meat. Jake circled nervously nearby, his ears flattened and his tail tucked between his legs.

"Is there anything I can do to help?"

Granda glanced up at her, then spat into the hay. Rainwater was dropping from the slats of the barn ceiling and kicking up little tufts of steam when it landed on the animal's hot back.

"Tis a bloody business, you know. Your own mother

wouldn't go near a cow calving. Made her dizzy."

"Well," Breda said, turning over a bucket and sitting next to him. "Kittens aren't *always* just like their cats."

"Fair enough," he said, though he looked unconvinced.

"So how can I help?"

"Well, I s'pose you could run inside and fix me a cup of tea."

Breda sighed and did as she was told. Of course Granda wouldn't trust her to be able to do anything more.

21.

Back at the house, Breda made the tea and poured it into a thermos halfway filled with milk, the way Granda liked it. Then she ran back through the rain puddles, the flashlight bouncing light in one hand, the tea in the other. She couldn't have been gone more than ten minutes, but something in the air had changed. The shed was thick with a sharp, bloody smell. The cow's eyes rolled, her mouth frothed; she kicked and shuffled in her pen.

"Does this mean it's close?" She handed Granda his tea, hoping she'd managed to keep the trembling out of her voice.

"The crubeens are out. Come closer, Breda."

She stepped forward. Granda pointed, and then she saw them, hanging out from under the cow's tail: two pink, spindly legs.

"Won't be long now," he said grimly, and Breda felt her own skinny legs buckle with relief. She didn't know how much longer she could watch and listen to this animal's suffering.

But despite Granda's prediction, as the cow's cries increased, as the foam spat and flew from her mouth, the little crubeens hung unmoving beneath her tail.

"Something's wrong," Granda finally said. He pulled on a long yellow glove, the kind they used at home for cleaning out the sinks at the salon. And then, without any warning, he lifted the cow's tail and reached in. She screamed now, kicking wildly, as Granda dodged her hooves and stared up in concentration at the beamed ceiling, feeling inside.

"You're hurting her!" Breda cried.

"It can't be helped," he answered, and, with an awful sucking sound, pulled his hand out. The glove emerged covered with slime and blood. "The calf is turned."

"Turned?"

"Breeched."

"Maybe we should call a vet or something?"

"We will do no such thing," he snapped. "I always done this meself and I've no notion of changing my ways now."

He reached down again and stuck his hand back inside. The cow bellowed, and Breda had to look away.

"'Tis turned arse over teakettle and stuck in the birthing

canal. And thanks to this blasted arthritis, I can't grab ahold of it to right it." Granda pulled his arm out for the second time, unpeeled the glove with his free hand, and threw it across the shed. "Blast it!"

"Let me try."

The words were out of Breda's mouth before she even knew she'd thought them. Of course she couldn't try. She eyed the discarded glove, lying in the hay, slick with blood and mucus.

"Don't be thick. You wouldn't have a clue what to do."

"Then teach me."

"I haven't bloody time to—" The cow screamed again, and crashed against the side of its pen.

"It's either that, or call the vet! She sounds like she's going to die!"

Granda watched Breda in the flickering half-darkness given off by his lantern. "Alright, so," he sighed, and handed her the remaining clean glove in the pair. "Take this."

She pulled the glove up over her elbow.

"Now. In a good birth, the front legs come first. Those legs we see—the crubeens—I thought those *were* the front two, but now I see that they're the back legs. So what we need is to push them back inside and turn the calf so its front legs come out first. What you'll do now is put your hand inside and feel for the head."

"But how will I know where it is?"

"Because it will feel like a bloody head! When you find a good place to grip, you'll start to turn it round, as slow and gentle as you can. And if you can do that, the cow should do the rest herself. She just needs a little help is all."

"Okay." Breda's voice was flat and assured, even though her legs were shaking. *You can only learn by doing*, her mom liked to say, although she was referring to the first time she'd ever cut a pair of bangs, not the first time she ever helped save a screaming cow's life by turning a breeched calf in its birth canal. Breda placed a hand on the laboring cow's flank. Even through the thick layer of her rubber glove, she could feel the heat of the cow's skin. Granda held the tail to the side. "Sorry," she whispered, and plunged her hand inside. The cow bellowed and bucked, but Granda stood right next to Breda, guarding her from its kicks. Inside the cow's body she could feel it—a trembling baby, so close to entering the world but not quite able to get the rest of the way.

"What's going on in there?" Granda demanded. "Tell me what you feel."

Her hand found bones, wetness, a familiar roundness and a thin rope of muscle and wet hair.

"I think I'm touching its butt."

"Right so. Blast it. That's what I thought. Alright now, as gentle as you can, I want you to push the arse toward me, like you're winding the hands of a clock."

Breda took a deep breath, gripped the calf's body, and twisted. The crubeens were sucked back inside the cow, who howled and kicked. Granda now placed his hand above Breda on the cow's miserable, shivering flank and spoke quietly to the animal: "Now, old girl. It's alright. Steady on. Now, now, girl. Steady on." It was as gently as she'd ever heard him speak to anyone.

"Go on," he ordered Breda. "Keep turning it. Go *on*, Breda."

Breda was aware of the tears that were pouring down her face. The cow's screams sounded so terrifyingly human.

"I can't," she whimpered. "It's not working!"

"Go *on*, Breda! Stop your whingeing! There is nothing worse than beginning a thing and giving up before you see it through."

Breda wiped her eyes with her free hand and continued to turn. Relentlessly but gently, the way she imagined the turning of a giant ship. And suddenly, the baby inside its mother seemed to give, the clock hand was turning, and a pressure was being released.

"I think I turned it!" she shouted.

"Fantastic!"

She turned to him, beaming, her hand still holding on to the calf inside its mother. "I did it, Granda! I did it!"

"Self praise is no praise, child! Now get your hand out of that bloody cow and leave her at it!"

She did as she was told, feeling both euphoric and chastened, and unpeeled the goo-covered glove, tossing it away as Granda had. Together they watched as the cow leaned against one of the walls of the pen. A great shiver passed through her, from her head down through her swollen body and all the way to her limp tail. She dug her huge wet nose into the hay and buckled her knees. A cloud of steam appeared in the cold air. The cow lifted her face to the ceiling of the barn and grew very still and silent. And all the while Granda talked to her in a quiet gentle voice.

The calf slipped out, first the crubeens, then the head, and then the rest of him, steaming, into the hay, followed by a gush of hot murky water that splashed all over Breda's wellies and pants. The whole barn smelled, suddenly, of the sea. The calf had been born. The cow now stamped her feet and whinnied, as if a bit embarrassed she'd just made such a fuss. The calf tried to make a sound, but when it opened its mouth, a shimmering bubble of saliva filled and popped. The cow turned around, nudged her baby closer, and then went to work cleaning its coat with her thick, papery tongue. The calf closed its filmy eyes and basked in the force of its mother's first touch.

Granda laughed a little as he walked out of the barn, returning a few minutes later carrying a cold bottle of beer for himself and a can of Club Orange for Breda. He uncapped the bottle with his teeth.

"Breda my girl," he said, clinking his bottle against her soda, "you're as handy as a small pot."

Breda sipped her drink to cover up the huge smile spreading across her face.

"He's a fine little calf, so he is." He patted Breda on the shoulder, his thick, clumsy fingers curling around her jacket. "You did a fine job. If you hadn't come in and saved the day, we may have lost both mother and calf."

"No way. You would have called the vet if it got any worse."

"How little you know me, child." He made a noise of disgust. "I'd rather lose my whole herd than ring up that eejit asking for help. Twas you, Breda. *You* saved the day."

Breda lowered her eyes. This was better, a million times better, than winning that writing contest. She felt so proud and happy.

"So what are you going to call the young fella, anyway?"

Granda took a long drink of his beer.

"I thought you said we weren't supposed to name the livestock."

"Your mother, when she was young, had a name for every cow in the herd." He smiled at her over the top of his bottle, his eyes crinkling. "Briseann an dúchais, trí shúil an chat."

"Alright," she said, and thought about it for a minute. "How about Bo?"

"Hm. That's quite an interesting name."

"You like it?"

"D'you know what bó means in Irish, do you?"

She shook her head.

"*Cow.*"

He looked down at her, his blue eyes crinkling again.

"Wait," she said. "So I just named a cow, Cow?"

"You did indeed."

They both burst out laughing at the same time. It felt wonderful to finally laugh along with Granda. The soft brown creature nuzzling his mother inside the pen had changed something between the two of them. She had proved to Granda that she could be useful, that she could be brave and strong, that she had farmer's blood running through her veins that even a lifetime in Chicago hadn't been able to erase.

It was very late now and the rain kept falling. They finished their drinks and left the mother and her new baby to sleep against each other in the cozy pen. Breda collapsed into her own bed and fell asleep, still smiling, as soon as her head hit the pillow.

22.

WHEN BREDA WOKE UP THE NEXT MORN-
ing, the sky was clear and the pastures glittered
green. She ate her toast and oatmeal alone while Granda slept
off their late night. When she was finished eating, she washed
her bowl and spoon, then walked down to the barn to check
on Bo. Granda said he would give the new calf and his mother
some time to rest and recover, and after that, they'd be turned
out into the field with the rest of the herd. At first, this seemed
a bit cruel to Breda, but when she drew the bolt on the gate and
walked into the dim, sweet-smelling barn, she saw that the little
calf was already walking on his own, circling the pen on impos-
sibly skinny legs. He wasn't even wobbling.

Breda started walking toward the pen, but before she could

get close, Bo's mother stomped a warning with her back hoof, swishing her tail and tossing her head from side to side. She snorted a puff of hot air through her huge nostrils, until Breda took a few steps back. Breda longed to reach through the slats and run her hand along Bo's soft fur, but his mother's message was clear—stay back and don't touch.

"Hey, Bo," she cooed instead, squatting down and waving at the little creature. He had glossy, nut-brown fur, a constellation of small white spots across his flanks, and big dark liquid eyes like his mother. He glanced at her with mild curiosity, twitching one ear, before returning to his mother's milk. Breda stood there, watching. Even if she couldn't touch him, it felt good just to be near him, to soak up the warm mother love that filled their cozy little corner of the shed.

She had returned from the barn and was just climbing on her bike to go for a ride when Granda emerged from the house with Jake following close behind. He held a large wicker basket in one hand, and a faded wool blanket was draped over his other arm.

"You going on a picnic, Granda?"

"That will have to wait until later," he said, pointing at her bike and ignoring her question. "Today we've got something to do."

Without further explanation, he headed toward the gravel

path. By now, Breda understood what this meant: that she was expected to follow him, and that she was not entitled to ask any more questions. She wheeled her bike back inside the main shed and jogged past the barn to catch up. Together they ducked under an electric fence to reach the bottom of the steep green hill where the digger was parked. He pulled open the squeaky door and motioned for Breda to climb in, with Jake hopping up behind her. Inside, the cab smelled like diesel and leftover sandwich rinds. The key was already in the ignition. When Granda turned it, the whole machine began to growl, and as they chugged up the steep incline, Breda had to hold on to the hot vinyl edges of her seat—there was no seat belt—aware of the soft green earth turning beneath its wide treads.

"At the top of this hill is a river," called Granda. She was sitting right next to him in the stuffy cab, but she could barely hear him over the roar of the engine. "Once you cross to the far side of it, you've reached the eastern border of our land." Breda pressed her fingers against the glass as she listened, watching the digger make its slow progress up the hill.

"Now, I was no oil painting, even in my younger days," he continued. "So most of the time I don't mind growing old. The wrinkles and the white hair, it don't bother me. And I'm not nearly as quick to anger as I was when I was a younger man."

At this, Breda stifled a laugh. So the version of Granda she was getting—this was the *mellowed* version? Still, he was being uncharacteristically chatty this morning. She glanced down at the wicker basket he'd placed at her feet, and, with her toe, carefully pushed the lid to one side. Inside, she saw some grapes and a sleeve of biscuits, two rolled linen napkins. *Had* Granda actually packed a picnic? For her? For the two of them? She pushed the lid back into place, deciding it was better to say nothing—she was afraid of breaking this sudden spell of kindness.

"But there's one thing I *detest* about growing old," he went on. "I can't climb this hill no more. Used to do it nearly every day, rain or shine. Used to bring your mother up here when she was a girl. A few years ago, the arthritis slowed me down, and then the stent in my heart put an end to my climbing days for good. Now I've got to drive wherever I need to go, like a lazy American."

Breda chewed her lip but did not respond. She knew that one of Granda's favorite ways to irritate her mother was to make jabs about Americans, and she wasn't going to take the bait. After that, he was silent. When they had nearly reached the crest of the hill, Granda cut the engine and stepped out. He came around to the other side, opened Breda's door, and extended a hand.

"Tis a short climb to the top, and we'll hoof the rest of it," he said, reaching past her to grab the blanket and the basket as she jumped down to the ground. "If I can't manage even that, you may as well put me out to grass, by God."

"Where are we going? What's at the top?"

"Tagann grásta Dé le foighne, child. Patience wins the grace of God."

As they climbed, Granda had to stop frequently for breath. When Breda tried to ask him if he was okay, he waved her off, and told her he was only stopping so he could teach a clueless city Yank like her about the various plants and trees growing wild along the hillside—bright yellow bunches of furze, delicate pink dog roses with velvety heart-shaped petals, and cascading green bunches of maidenhair fern. He showed her the bird cherry tree, with its spindly, leaf-thick branches and shiny dark berries, and peeled off a patch of its bark, holding it under her nose to smell. She backed away, gagging.

"Not what you were expecting, eh?" Granda said.

"It reminds me of garbage pickup day in Chicago."

"In ancient times," he explained, tossing the bark into the brush, Jake bolting after it, "peasants would peel off this bark and hang it over their doorways. Believed the stink would ward off plague. I s'pose you can guess how well *that* worked."

They moved on to a stand of huge, beautiful trees, listing seaward, puffed out with great bunches of fluttering leaves. "And here we have the aspen. At this size, I'd say this thicket is hundreds of years old. See how their leaves tremble in the wind?"

Breda looked up at the white-bottomed leaves that shook delicately, emitting a low whispering sound.

"This is because, you see, aspen wood was used to build the cross where Christ was crucified. And because of that, these trees are destined to tremble with shame for all eternity. Or so they say."

Breda looked up. It was true—the leaves of the trees shivered and shook, as if filled with fear or regret.

"Who's 'they'?" she asked. But Granda did not answer.

At last they neared the top of the great hill, and when Breda turned and looked back, her stomach dropped at the dizzying view below. The farmhouse, from this vantage, looked no larger than a square of white cotton.

"Now." Granda stood next to her, breathing heavily as he pinched out a wad of tobacco from his tin. "What d'you make of our land?"

Breda took a deep breath. All around her, the world was white and blue and green, with little bursts of pink and lavender and yellow from the flowers. They were too high above the farm now for the wind to carry the more domestic odors of the livestock and sheds. She had never breathed air this clean.

"It's beautiful," she whispered.

"Yes, well." He arranged the tobacco in his cheek. "Tis a pity you can't eat the scenery. If you could, perhaps the millions of our people who emigrated would never have left." They were both quiet then, and Breda wondered if he was thinking about her mother.

"This farm originally belonged to your grandmother, God rest her. She was an only child, you see, and so there were no sons to inherit it, as was the usual tradition. She died when your mother was small, as I'm sure you know. And so it was left to me. Before that, it belonged to her father, and his father, and his father's father. On and on." He worked at the tobacco in his cheek. "One day twill belong to you."

Breda stared at him. "To me?" she echoed, her voice faint.

"Sure, what'd you think, that I'd take this piece of ground your people have worked for centuries, and auction it off to the highest bidder?" he snapped, and the old grouchiness she'd come to know was almost a relief. What he'd just said . . . as they stood in this magnificent place . . . it was too much for Breda to feel all at once. Granda looked at her stunned face, his voice softening a little. "We're each of us only stewards, Breda, and so you may as well learn a thing or two about the history of this land and the things that grow here." He bent down suddenly and plucked a small white flower from the ground, handing it to her. "This, for example, is the Kerry lily. A beautiful little wildflower if there ever was one. It's fairly rare. It don't grow in any other part of the world. So don't ever let me catch you picking any."

As he handed her the delicate little flower, Breda held back a smile, as well as the urge to point out to Granda that *he* had just picked the Kerry lily. Instead she just nodded and tucked the stem behind her ear. He pointed to a formation of huge black rocks planted out in the far-off waves. "See those? You know what those are, do you?"

"The Blasket Islands?"

"Na Blascaodaí. Good. Inhabited for thousands of years by poets and fishermen. In the 1950s, the Irish government evacuated the last remaining few people who lived there. Now it's mostly chough and gray seals and abandoned cottages."

He turned abruptly and kept climbing. Breda followed close behind until she could hear the soft sound of rushing water, and Granda came to a stop.

"Now here," he said, breathing heavily, "is our river." They had reached the very top, where more huge trees grew along the riverbanks and the sun fell through their branches like golden confetti. "It runs through the edge of our farm, and out to the sea."

"Are these aspens too?" Breda asked.

"No, these are hazelnut trees. See?" He reached for a low

branch and pulled down a handful of green nuts. "Been a staple of our diets for thousands of years. Our ancient people even used to crush the leftover shells as carpets for their hovels. Ever taste one?"

She shook her head. He cracked one open with the broad end of his pocketknife and dropped the nut into Breda's palm. It was soft and buttery, with a satisfying crunch. The shards that caught between her teeth tasted earthy, almost chocolatey. He sent her to gather some more for their picnic, and when she'd filled her pockets and returned, Granda had rolled out the wool blanket, unloaded the wicker basket, and arranged lunch—grapes, digestive biscuits, wedges of yellow and white cheddar, and crackers. He handed her a cold can of Club Orange, and Breda took a long drink while he began cracking the nuts and placing them on a cloth napkin.

"Breda," he said, easing himself slowly to a sitting position on the blanket as he popped a grape into his mouth, "did you ever hear the story of the Salmon of Knowledge?"

Breda reached up to touch her ear, to make sure her Kerry lily was still in place. "No, Granda."

"Well," he said, clearing his throat, pressing his shoulders back, his voice already deepening as he assumed the manner of the seanchaí, "I s'pose it's about time you did."

23.

"**M**ANY THOUSANDS OF YEARS AGO," HE began, "when our people were fisher-gatherers living in wattled houses along the coasts, subsisting on seaweed, salmon, and these hazelnuts here, before Ireland was Ireland, it was called Eire, an island of clans named for the mother goddess. In this time and place, there lived a band of warriors called the Fianna. They were the bravest, smartest, and strongest soldiers in the land. Joining the Fianna was every young child's dream, but as you might imagine, it was very difficult to achieve.

"In order to even begin training, you must pass a series of very difficult tests: First, you had to fight ten men carrying spears, while you yourself were armed with nothing but a stick. Next, you had to run through a forest in absolute silence, without so much as snapping a twig or rustling a leaf. And lastly, you had to know, by heart, all the poetry of all the clans—because soldiers in the time of Eire were not simply brute warriors, but learned men and women who understood that strength without wisdom is both useless and dangerous. They understood that you must be both poet and warrior, cat and wolf, fox and badger."

Breda leaned back on the blanket and closed her eyes, letting the dappled sun warm her face. She relaxed her body, slipping into Granda's tale like a stone being pulled into the ocean by the tide.

"During this time, there lived a young boy by the name of Fionn Mac Cumhaill. Fionn's father, Cumhall, had been one of the greatest Fianna warriors ever to live. But Fionn never knew his father, who'd been killed in a battle while Fionn was still growing in his mother's belly. Even so, his greatest dream was to follow in Cumhall's footsteps. The problem was, Fionn was his mother's whole world, her only child, and she did not want to send him away, even for an honor as great as that. But she also knew, as the saying goes, that a child's got to do his own growing, no matter how tall his father.

"And so on the day Fionn reached about the same age as your own, his mother sent him away to live with the great teacher Finnegas and study the ways of the Fianna. Finnegas lived

on the banks of a river, just like the one you see before you."
Granda swept his hand over the land, and Breda felt a shiver
zipping up her spine. It was as if the soft cadence of his voice had
the power to collapse thousands of years like an accordion, and
the rough wool of the blanket fell away beneath her as the rooks
cackled in the hazelnut trees, calling her away to the ancient
place and time of the story.

"Twas here on the riverbank that Finnegas taught Fionn
nearly everything he knew. How to hunt and fish and trap, how
to gather wild honey and elderberries from the forest, how to
dive for crab and mussels. How to cook and prepare food, how
to spin wool and sew clothes, how to care for children and the
elderly, how to fight with fist and spear. In those days, there
was no such thing as 'men's work' or 'women's work.' There
was only work, and Fionn learned how to do all of it, capably
and well. Finnegas taught Fionn to move like a panther through
the woods and hills, soundless, listening, seeing everything.
He taught Fionn how poetry is built, line by line, how it can
transform difficult feelings into language as though by magic.
But he also taught Fionn how to break his enemy's neck, killing him dead before he'd even known he'd been attacked. He
taught Fionn how to weave tapestries using fine gold threads
and crushed indigo, but he also taught him how to skin and gut
a red deer, and to use every part of the carcass, right down to

whittling a spear from its bleached bones.

"But there was one piece of knowledge which Finnegas hid from his young pupil and kept for himself. There was a reason why Finnegas, who was born in the north, had chosen to journey for days by donkey over craggy broken land, and set up his camp on this *particular* river, in this *particular* spot, surrounded by *these* nine hazelnut trees."

Breda opened her eyes and looked above her. It was true: there stood, on the banks of the river, exactly nine trees—five on one side, and four on the other. Wasn't this supposed to be a legend, a fairy tale? So why did it feel so real?

"You see, Breda, Finnegas knew something no one else did: that all the wisdom of the whole universe existed in the nuts of these nine hazelnut trees. In the first tree lived everything there was to know about love. In the second, all there was to know about death. In the third, the mysteries of the planets, the galaxies, and the universe. In the fourth, the secrets of the animals. The fifth, the knowledge of water and air. In the sixth, fire and earth. The seventh tree contained everything there was to know about human beings. And in the eighth, all there was to know about the fairies, and all the other things that live flitting around among us unseen. The ninth and final tree contained every answer to every prayer and wish and silent plea that had ever been uttered.

"One night, many years before Finnegas set up his camp here on the river, a terrible thunderstorm swept across the whole island, from the northern islands of Donegal to the very southernmost tip of Cork. The winds howled as they had never howled before, shaking each and every hazelnut from all the trees of knowledge. They splashed like hail into the choppy river. Now at the time, a great silver salmon lived in this river. As the storm raged, this fish swam from bank to bank, swallowing every single hazelnut from each of the nine trees. In this way, the great silver salmon came to possess all the knowledge of the universe, of love and death and life, of people and plants and animals, of all the seen and unseen elements of the world, of the dirt and worms beneath our feet all the way out to the stars in our sky and the stars beyond those stars that we can't see or name.

"And what Finnegas knew, which he did not tell Fionn, was that any man or woman who caught this Salmon of Knowledge and ate of its flesh would come to own all the knowledge of the universe, too. And this was Finnegas the Teacher's obsession and greatest desire.

"Every morning, when the sky was still black-purple and young Fionn still slept, Finnegas would walk out of his hut and down to the banks of the river. He would cast his line in search of the great salmon—but he never could catch it. It would be some job, wouldn't it, trying to catch a fish that's a thousand times smarter than you could ever hope to be? The fish enjoyed toying with Finnegas, in fact. It often took the bait, leaving the hook, and splashed away, as if laughing at Finnegas. And it drove Finnegas stone mad.

"But one morning young Fionn awoke early. He completed all his morning chores swiftly, and rather than sitting about idly, he asked if he could help Finnegas with the fishing. And it occurred to Finnegas, who was so tired of failure, that perhaps the strength of the young warrior might be just the thing for catching the great fish. And indeed, that very day, they had a stroke of luck: they hooked the fish straight through its gills—which meant it could not wriggle away so easily. Finnegas, with the help and strength of the young boy, battled and battled for hours. The line nearly broke, their legs and arms burned, but slowly, slowly, teacher and pupil dragged the fish onto the bank. It flapped furiously in the grass, its mouth opening and closing, its gills working like sails, its beautiful silver skin gleaming in the sun. But even a fish with all the knowledge of the universe has its physical limitations. And after a valiant battle on the bank of the river, the beautiful creature went still at last.

"'Boy!' Finnegas shouted. 'Build a fire and set the fish to cook. I must rest now—wake me when the fish is ready, and we will share this meal. But you must promise not to take even a single bite until I say so. The first taste of this fish belongs to me and me alone.'

"Fionn agreed quickly to this promise, for Finnegas had never shouted at him in this way, with eyes so wild. Finnegas went inside the hut to rest his aching bones, and Fionn built a great fire. He placed the salmon on sticks, and began to turn it carefully over the flames. His stomach roared—the fish smelled wonderful as its skin began to crackle with fat and heat. But Fionn was good and honest and true to his promise: he dared not take even one bite.

"But then, in the heat of the flame, a blister began to rise on the skin of the fish. Without thinking, Fionn reached out to pop the blister, and in doing so, he burned the pad of his thumb. To ease the pain, he stuck his thumb in his mouth and sucked at where the fat had burned his skin. Immediately, his heart and mind began to fill, for he had tasted the Salmon of Knowledge and all the wisdom of the universe now belonged to him.

"When Finnegas awoke, he took one look at Fionn, at the brightness burning in the young warrior's eyes, and knew that it was too late—his pupil had tasted the salmon first. When Fionn explained what had happened, Finnegas could not even be angry.

"'Twas meant to be,' Finnegas said sadly. 'Go, boy, now, and live. For there is nothing more that I can teach you.' As always,

Fionn obeyed his teacher's instructions. He left Finnegas's camp that very day, setting off into the wide world, and went on to become the greatest warrior-poet of all time."

Breda was quiet for a moment, watching the river and the hazelnut trees moving in the wind, the aspen trembling with their ancient shame.

"Granda?"

"Aye?"

"Is that story really true?"

"You're asking the wrong question, child." He sipped his thermos of tea. "Truth is a thing more slippery than a fish. That's something you'll learn soon enough."

She drank her Club Orange, let the sugary bubbles cool her throat, and wondered what he meant by that.

"That fish we served you on your first night in Ballyglass," he went on, squinting out at the water, "I caught myself, from this river, for you. Now, I'm just a lowly old farmer. I haven't the wisdom of Finnegas, or the bravery of Fionn, for that matter. But even so, I am your blood, Breda, and if only you listen, there are many things that I can teach you."

Breda wanted to say something kind to Granda then. She wanted to promise him that she would grow up to be a good steward of their land—that she would honor and care for the plants and trees and river, the cows and their calves, the house and all its outbuildings. But she already understood that Granda didn't do those kinds of conversations. He didn't talk about feelings, except through his stories. So instead, she put down her drink, scooted closer to him, and leaned her head against his shoulder. At first he stiffened, like a frightened deer. But then he relaxed again, and behind his thermos of tea, Breda could see he was almost smiling.

24.

AFTER THE BIRTH OF BO AND THEIR TRIP to the river, things were different between Breda and Granda. He still didn't say much, but when he did, his voice was softer and he looked her in the eye. He even sometimes laughed with her. And though this made her happy in a deep and quiet way she found hard to explain, there was just one problem: she'd already promised Nellie Fahey she would come back for football training, and it was a lot easier to betray Granda's wishes when he'd treated her like an annoying pest instead of a real granddaughter—instead of the girl who he would one day entrust with his beloved farm. Still, she thought, maybe it was wrong to disobey him, but was it as wrong as letting her whole lifetime go by without a visit or a birthday card or a phone call? Was it *her* fault she'd had to wait nearly thirteen years to have a relationship with him? No, she told herself firmly. It certainly wasn't. And so, the next Friday, Breda spent the afternoon reading in the slow, quiet peace of the barn across from Bo and his mother, and in the early evening, she pushed the guilt away, climbed onto her bike, and rode toward Castlemaine.

Nellie was there again, and Seamus, and most of the other cousins and friends who'd been there the previous week. But this time, they weren't underestimating Breda as a clueless Yank who'd never touched a Gaelic football before. When they broke off into teams, Roddie, the under-16s trainer, put her in the forward position where she would have ample opportunities to try to score. The whistle blew and the other team marked her closer this time around, chased her harder, treated her as a threat. And it worked. Again and again she was beaten to the ball. She only had time and space to set up for a shot once, and when she tried to kick the ball over the bar for a point, Saoirse, who could jump much higher than her skinny legs suggested, leaped up and stuffed it back to the ground. By the time Seamus shouldered Breda out of the way to catch a pass and she found herself lying flat on her back, the wind knocked out of her lungs and tears stinging her eyes, she had half a mind to limp back to her bike and ride home. *I never should have disobeyed him*, she thought. *I never should have come.*

When the whistle blew for halftime, Nellie linked a sweaty arm through Breda's and drew her aside.

"Alright, Yank?"

"Yeah." Breda winced, breathing deeply through the cramp in her side.

"Thought we'd go easy on ya after the way you hustled us last week?"

"I didn't *hustle* anybody."

"You scored a point off Saoirse, one of the best players on our team. We weren't expecting that, were we?" Nellie shot Breda a lopsided smile as she handed her a water bottle. Breda gulped some down and rubbed the sore place on her shoulder where Seamus had knocked into her.

"Hey, take it as a compliment. We know you're good, so we ain't going easy on you. Just push harder and don't take nothing from nobody, my big brother most of all."

"Okay." The cramp was working its way out of her muscles, and she was starting to feel a little better.

"You got this, Breda. Yeah?"

"Yeah," Breda said, meeting Nellie's friendly eyes, her face setting into a determined smile. "Yeah, I do."

The whistle blew on the second half and Breda jogged out to the pitch. Nellie's pep talk had reenergized her. She *would* push harder. Just because this was a casual scrimmage didn't mean she shouldn't try her best. She held steady for most of the second half—not making any plays, but not messing anything up, either. And then, just before the final whistle blew, while the evening sun sparkled above the Atlantic, one of the Fahey cousins—Elaine or Eileen; she couldn't remember which was which—passed her the ball. Seamus, all six feet of him, came barreling toward her. She knew she couldn't fight him; but a summer of bike riding had made her legs strong and quick— maybe she could outrun him. She dodged right, then tacked left and squeaked past him, leaving him cursing and grabbing at air. From there, the pitch was wide open. But she knew the rules: players couldn't run more than four steps without passing, bouncing, or soloing the ball. She ran her four steps, bounced and caught the ball, ran four more, and looked around desperately for someone to pass to—she knew she didn't have the skills to solo, which was a tricky move. But she'd outrun everyone, even her own teammates, and there was no one close enough to take her pass.

"Shoot, Yank!" She heard Nellie, and other teammates, screaming behind her. The net was there, the goalkeeper was

Niall, and he was shuffling back and forth, his arms spread wide. She could try for the crossbar, an easier score worth fewer points. But she was close enough to the goal to see Niall's face, and he looked scared. Of her. She dropped the ball and kicked it with all her might. It shot forward and sailed straight past Niall's waving arms, into the net for a goal. He buried his face in his keeper's gloves, while Breda's team went crazy. They had won the match.

Breda made her way through the throng of her hugging, high-fiving teammates. Even Niall, a good sport, jogged over to congratulate her.

"Well done, Yank," he said, glumly holding out a hand for her to shake.

"Well done, indeed," Nellie laughed, grinning as she slapped Breda on the back. "My uncle's coming round to collect us— we'll tell him about our glorious victory and maybe he'll take us for a ninety-nine."

"A ninety-nine?" Breda asked.

"An ice cream cone, like. He'll give you a drive home afterward."

"Oh, I don't think—" Breda could almost picture the look on Granda's face when a Fahey vehicle came barreling up his drive to drop home his only grandchild.

"Ah! There he is now."

She pointed as a mud-caked white work van pulled up to the edge of the field, and Breda watched a tall man with red-blond hair and rubber knee boots climb out and walk toward the pitch. When he got close enough that she could make out his handsome features, Nellie drop-kicked the football in his direction. He bent his knees, squared up, and headed it back in a perfectly directed shot. Breda caught the ball and held it in her two hands.

"How'd it go, Tadgh?"

Nellie's uncle ran a hand through his thick hair. "Managed to save most of them. Had to put down five. I s'pose it could've been a lot worse."

"My uncle Tadgh here is the local vet," Nellie explained to Breda, sipping from her Lucozade. Breda nodded. So *that* was why Granda hadn't called the vet to help with Bo's birth: because the vet was a Fahey. "He was just dealing with a flock of sick sheep."

"Was it braxy?" Breda asked, remembering Granda's tale about the banshee holding the lamb. The Faheys stared at her for a moment in shock before they all burst out laughing.

"Sure you must be the first Chicago kid I ever met who's heard of braxy," Nellie said, giggling.

"A sheep ain't gonna get braxy in the summer," Seamus added, shaking his head and smirking. "They get it from grazing on frozen grass."

Breda felt her cheeks reddening.

"Ah, leave the girl alone," Tadgh said. "She was only making conversation, so she was." He smiled kindly at Breda. "Twas maggots that got the poor fellas."

"Oh."

"Tadgh, can you squeeze Breda in for a lift home?" asked Nellie. She smiled slyly before adding, "And maybe a ninety-nine?"

"I don't need one, but thanks," Breda said quickly. "I've got my bike with me."

"Ah, go on," said Nellie. "You won the match for us; the least we could do is buy you an ice cream."

"Another time, I promise."

"How long you in Dingle, Breda?" Tadgh asked.

"Oh, um. Just another week or so," she lied.

"You should take her out to the clochán," he said to Nellie. He turned to Breda. "The beehive huts. On the way out to Slea Head, near Ventry."

"Nah," Seamus said, waving his hand. "That old stuff is boring. Not everyone's a history nerd like yourself, Uncle Tadgh."

"Don't listen to this one," Tadgh said, thumbing in Seamus's direction and winking at Breda. "The clochán are older than any of those grand crumbling castles you see in the tour guides. And in better condition, too. Not to mention, they're *our* history, built by *our* people—not by English invaders."

"Here we go," sighed Seamus. "Hey, Tadgh, ever wonder if maybe you stopped talking so much about Irish history and animal diseases, you might actually have a girlfriend?"

"Everyone should see them when they're here," Tadgh went on, ignoring him. "My mate is one of the caretakers; he can even show you around."

"You mean to tell me Mícheál Sullivan's working at the huts now?" laughed Nellie. "Just last week he was at An Bradán. Will that man *ever* hold a steady job for more than a minute?"

Tadgh shrugged. "Hard work," he said, "has never been his specialty."

"Mícheál Sullivan?" The name was out of Breda's mouth before she realized she was speaking. "You mean the cook?"

Nellie gave her a funny look. "You know him?"

"Uh—well, I met him a couple weeks ago. I was at An Bradán with my—with my family."

"That's him." Tadgh nodded. "He should be up at the huts this Sunday. I can take the lot of ye, if you like."

This is my chance, thought Breda: to see Mícheál Sullivan on her own, without Noeleen or Granda there to stop her from asking questions. To stop her from asking *the* question. To stop her from finding out the truth.

"That actually sounds great," she said. "I'd love to."

"Tis a plan, then." Tadgh smiled. "Let's all meet Sunday. Half past three. The height of the Ventry road, beneath the Páidí Ó Sé statue. You can't miss it; tis about seven feet tall and made of bronze."

25.

TWO DAYS LATER, A GAGGLE OF FAHEYS waited for Breda beneath the bronze statue of Páidí Ó Sé, County Kerry's greatest Gaelic footballer, pushing and shoving and laughing in a way that made her yearn, as she often did, for a few siblings and cousins of her own. Breda loved that she and her mom were a team, but they *were* a very small team—a duo, more like—and sometimes she wondered whether being part of a big family like the Faheys meant that you could never be lonely. It sure seemed that way.

"You made it, Breda!" Nellie called, releasing her younger cousin, Jane, from the playful headlock she'd been holding her in. "Tadgh'll just be a minute, he's dealing with a horse crisis."

"Everything okay?" Breda hooked her chin over to where

Nellie's uncle's truck was parked at the side of the road. He was sitting in the driver's seat with his phone pressed to his ear, shouting something at the person on the other end of the line.

"Uncle T takes it personally when people who should know better let their animals get sick with perfectly preventable illnesses. The whole Donoghue herd has rain rash. Which could have all been avoided if someone'd bothered to rub them down with vegetable oil before that stormy spell we had last week. Speaking of." Nellie pointed up at the sky, where black clouds had begun scudding and rolling from the sea, gathering over the little town like enormous water balloons ready to burst. "Let's find a dry place to stash that bike."

The girls walked past the statue and down the short path that led into the village. They found a covered stone archway connecting two shops and pushed Breda's blue bike into the slotted shadow between a pair of gray crumbling walls. As soon as they were finished clipping her helmet onto her handlebars, a low moan of thunder rattled down the alleyway and a cold, wet wind gusted up around them. They ran back and climbed into Tadgh's truck behind Seamus, Jane, and Eileen just as the water-balloon clouds exploded and the rain began rushing down.

The western road out of Ventry toward the beehive huts hugged the ocean. Breda tried not to look out the window at the wide Atlantic raging and foaming against the edge of the rocks, like a vicious dog straining at its chain. She made a mental note to ask Granda whether a storm had ever come through Dingle so bad that the water breached the roads. But nobody else seemed concerned. They just sang along to Radio Kerry while Tadgh navigated the soaking hairpin road, windshield wipers flapping at top speed, one hand resting on the gearshift.

"Where did you say you were from, love?" he called to the back, glancing at Breda in the rearview.

"Chicago," Nellie answered for her. "When I do my J-1 summer over there, now I'll have someone to bunk with."

Breda laughed. She remembered her mother talking about the J-1 summer. Irish college kids got special visas to travel to the US to work in hotels and beachfront restaurants and construction sites for the summer. *I always wanted to do something like that*, her mom had said. *But I had you instead, and my carefree days were over.*

"Chicago." Tadgh nodded. "Great town."

"Sure, when were *you* ever in Chicago, Uncle T?" demanded Seamus. "Dad says you've hardly ever left Kerry."

"Well, I always meant to." He grinned, shaking his head. "I suppose I'll get there one day."

"There they are!" called Jane, squashed all the way in the back among Tadgh's veterinary instruments. She was pointing up toward the top of a roadside hill, jagged with rocky out-croppings. The giant rocks were black from rain, and the surrounding grass was a neon, verdant green. Dotted along the hill, like hunched little men, was a series of rounded stone huts built neatly of flat gray stones, each about as big as a small car.

Tadgh pulled off to the side of the road, and as soon as he cut the engine, Nellie whooped, grabbed Breda's hand, and pulled her out the door. Breda yanked her jacket hood over her head with her free hand, tightening the strings, and tried to look around for any sign of Mícheál Sullivan. But the wind was whipping up the rain so much it was like trying to look at the hill through smudged glass. She held on to Nellie's hand, and the girls ran together up the rocky path and ducked inside the doorway of the first little hut, just as another peal of thunder rocked the air.

Inside, the acoustics of the ancient structure transformed the sound of the storm into something strange and gentle—almost human, like thousands of lips parting over and over again. It was dark in there, nearly pitch black, and perfectly dry. Breda crouched down—the curved ceiling was too low to stand all the way up, except right in the middle—and breathed in the smell of moss and mineral, the salty tang of the sea blowing in through the open doorway.

"How old are these things, anyway?" she asked, running a

hand along the cool dark stone.

"Haven't a clue." Nellie sat back on her heels in the packed dirt. "A thousand years? Two thousand? Fierce old, anyway. You can ask Tadgh. He'd know."

But Breda already knew who she would ask. She wished, suddenly, that Granda were here with her, that she hadn't had to lie to him again. He would know everything there was to know about who built these huts, and when, and why. He would know what technique the ancient stone-layer had used to slot all these rocks together so tightly without a smidge of mortar or concrete. He would be able to tell her if Fionn Mac Cumhaill spent nights here, back in another lifetime when the Fianna roamed the island, a band of warrior-poets. With his stories he could wake the clochán's long-dead inhabitants from sleeping, like a miner tapping his pick into the past. Only Granda, the seanchaí, had the power and the skill to coax ghosts out of history.

"Hey, Nellie?" Breda looked at her friend in the darkness, willing her voice to sound casual. "Did you say that guy—I think his name was Mícheál?—was going to show us around?"

"Sully?" Sitting with her head leaned back against the far wall, Nellie opened one eye. "Oh, he's not here, is he? Must not've shown up for work today. What a shocker." She laughed.

Breda laughed, too. Or tried to. "You said he was your uncle's friend, though, right?"

"Best mates since they were little boys. Why?"

Breda shrugged. "I was just curious."

"A lot of people around here don't like him very much," Nellie went on, and Breda was secretly grateful for her new friend's chatty ways. "But Tadgh says he believes in loyalty. And second chances. Third and fourth chances sometimes, even."

"Why don't people like him?"

"Ah, you know. They say he's lazy. Unreliable. And then there's the thing with his children."

Breda shivered, aware, suddenly, of how sodden her clothes and shoes were. "He has children?"

"Oh yeah. All over Dingle, as a matter of fact. Not that he takes much of an interest in any of them."

Breda could feel her legs weaken beneath her. She'd thought—no, *known*—that Mícheál Sullivan could be her father. But it had never even crossed her mind that maybe he had other kids, too. Maybe she *did* come from a big family after all. Maybe she had a whole web of relatives, real brothers and sisters, who'd been kept a secret all her life. Maybe all this time, she wasn't *meant* to be lonely.

"Wow," she managed, willing her voice to stop shaking. "He sounds like a real jerk."

Nellie shrugged. "Ah, I wouldn't sweat it, Yank," she said with a laugh. "After all, he's not *your* daddy, is he?"

Breda tried to think of a lighthearted response, but she was too stunned to speak. Her eyes filled with tears.

"Wait," Nellie said, looking up at her, suddenly serious. "*Is he?*"

Breda didn't answer. She scrambled to her feet, pulled her hood closer around her face, and ducked out through the door, straight into the wind.

"*Wait!*" she heard Nellie call.

But Breda kept going, tripping down the rocky hill toward the road. She'd been the fastest kid on the football pitch that Friday. Nobody could catch her now that she had a real reason to run.

26.

S HE HADN'T MADE IT VERY FAR DOWN THE
road before Tadgh's truck pulled up beside her. She kept
running, pretending she didn't see him. Her teeth were chatter-
ing so hard she could hear them clacking together, even over
the sound of the waves beyond the grass. He slowed to a crawl
and rolled down his window.

"C'mon, love," he said. "Hop in. You're soaked to the skin."

Great observation, she thought, and kept going, leaning into
the wind.

"You want to catch pneumonia? Is that it?"

Nellie's face appeared, squeezing into the window next to
her uncle's. "Get in, Breda," she shouted, "and stop with the
drama. These waves have been known to reach the road when it

rains like this." She nodded toward the ocean. "Fancy a swim do you?"

That stopped Breda in her tracks. Maybe Granda was right and the Faheys really were a bunch of criminals and liars. Maybe Nellie was lying to her right now. She glanced from beneath her hood at the writhing ocean. But it *did* seem kind of stupid, taking that chance. And anyway: if there was one thing Breda was *not*, would never be, it was a drama queen. Tadgh rolled to a stop and Seamus pushed open the back door for her. She sighed and climbed back in.

As soon as she was in the truck, it was clear that Nellie had already blabbed to everyone about what had happened in the hut. About Mícheál Sullivan. The Faheys were as awkward with silence as Granda was comfortable with it. Seamus and Nellie, in particular, looked like they were dying to say something. To ask her more questions. There was a lot of throat clearing and fake coughing. Tadgh just drove, looking straight ahead. But the back of his neck was all mottled red, like it embarrassed him just being around her.

When they reached the village, Tadgh parked on the main street and looked at her in his mirror.

"Nellie says you left your bicycle here?"

Breda nodded.

"We can put it in the back of the truck and I can drive you

the rest of the way to your B and B."

"No," Breda said, a little louder than she'd intended. But she'd had enough for one day, without having to picture Granda's reaction at a Fahey veterinary truck snaking up his driveway. "My—um—hotel is close by. Really."

He narrowed his eyes at her. But if he knew she was lying, he decided not to push it.

"Then at least let me help you get your bike back onto the road."

"Fine. Thanks." She unbuckled her seat belt in a hurry, as Nellie and the rest of the kids waved, murmuring their goodbyes, red-faced, giggling. Tadgh followed her down the alleyway where she'd stashed her bike, and she pointed it out to him in its hiding spot. He reached up, grabbed it by the handlebars, and pulled it out from between the two stone walls. The rain, she saw, had soaked his whole back, darkening his navy-blue soccer shirt.

"This is your bicycle?" he asked. He was still holding on to the handlebars, looking down at the shining blue frame.

"Yeah." She unhooked her helmet and clipped it beneath her chin. "Thank you for driving me."

He didn't say anything.

"So, um." She took the bike gently from his grip. "Bye."

He blinked at her for a moment, then nodded down the alley.

"Are you sure you won't let me take you the rest of the way? Still lashing out there."

"No, thank you." She swung her leg over the crossbar and bounced on her tires. Tadgh started to say something else, but whatever it was, it was lost in another crack of thunder. And Breda, feeling suddenly completely drained of emotion, didn't stick around to wait for him to repeat himself.

27.

BREDA RODE HOME INTO THE WIND, THE
rain stinging her face, nearly blinding her. When she
coasted down Granda's driveway, she could see his digger trun-
dling along halfway up the hill, turning earth for new grazing
land. She parked her dripping bike inside the shed and walked
out toward the barn.

Bo was there, like always, with his mother. In this quiet
place, with these quiet animals, Breda could already feel her
heart steadying. She leaned against the wall, watching them.
She would miss this so much when Granda eventually turned
them back out into the field. But for now, mother and baby
were safe in the barn, and they were so used to her presence
that Bo's mother didn't protest anymore, not even when Breda

crept closer to watch the little calf close his eyes and rest his head against her brown flank. Not even when she reached into the pen and stroked the bushy little switch at the end of his tail. Sliding down to sit on the floor, the boards warm beneath her wet jeans, Breda considered that maybe she'd been wondering her whole life about a father who never thought about her at all. She allowed herself to sit with that thought for a minute, and was a little surprised to discover that it didn't feel quite so awful. After all, she had one parent who loved her, who protected her, who had always been there for her, and always would be. Like Bo, Breda had been surrounded by love from the moment she was born. Even when her mother was working nonstop, even when she was sending Breda across the ocean to teach her a lesson, Breda could still feel that love. It never went away. And wasn't that enough?

Still, the question nagged at her. She had to know for sure, even if it was going to hurt. She could handle hard truths. She was tough, like her mother. Briseann an dúchais, trí shúil an chat.

Back at Granda's, a pot of vegetable soup was simmering on the stove, and the whole house was cozy with warmth and dryness and the smells of good, simple cooking. Breda stirred the pot, tasted a few bites from the big wooden spoon. She paced the long hallway. For a while she just sat in her bedroom and watched the rain. Then she walked back down to the kitchen and picked up the cordless phone. She returned to her bedroom, closed the door, and dialed.

"Breda!" Her mom picked up on the second ring. "I was just thinking about you this very minute."

"Hi, Mom. I was just thinking about you, too."

"I checked my weather app this morning. Looks like you've a wet week coming up."

"Yeah, it's pouring here now." She tucked the phone between her ear and chin and walked into her little bathroom to stand before the mirror and scrutinize her face, looking for signs of Mícheál Sullivan.

"Did I tell you what happened with Rita? You know, my regular who always comes in with that little dog of hers? Well, it turns out she went ahead and cheated on me with another stylist at some cheap salon out by the airport. And guess what happened? They gave her perm burn. So she had to come back to me, hat in hand, with a wretched peeling scalp and electric socket hair. She looked so sorry I couldn't even be angry with her. 'Maura,' she was wailing, 'please forgive me, I had a coupon!'"

Breda closed her eyes and took in the sound of her mother's laughter. "Were you able to fix it?"

"Took the whole of the afternoon yesterday. But I did, of course. I'm good at what I do, kiddo."

"Self praise is no praise, Mom."

"Oh Lord. I see your granda has taught you one of his favorite phrases. Say—speaking of, have you gotten to meet anyone your own age? Or is that cranky old man taking up all your time?"

"I did, actually. I've been playing football with a girl I met in the village."

"That's fantastic! Does this new friend have a name?"

Breda paused. "It's Nellie. Nellie Fahey."

"Nellie Fahey." It was more a statement than a question. Her voice had gone all soft and wistful—a voice Breda had never heard before. "She was only a baby when I left home. Mad. I can still picture that little shock of red hair."

"It's still red."

"Well, I s'pose it would be. Red like that doesn't fade, even when the child grows older." On the other end of the line, there was a long pause. "I have to say, I'm fairly shocked your granda allows it."

"Allows what?"

"Allows you to pal around with a Fahey."

"Well, that's the thing. He told me I could go anywhere on the peninsula except for Fahey's Pub. So I haven't exactly told him."

"Ah. Sneaking around behind his back, are you? I know a thing or two about that."

"But why does Granda hate them so much, anyway? What did they do that was so bad? He didn't really give me any details."

"How do I . . . see, your granda's had some disagreements with the family over the years. As he does with many people, in case you haven't noticed."

"So you're not gonna tell me any more than that."

"Well. There's no use boiling cabbage twice, is there? To borrow another one of his phrases."

"Mom?"

"Yes, love?"

"Do you know a man named Mícheál Sullivan?"

"Sully?" Her mom paused again. "I do. Though it's been years, of course. Why?"

"I think you know why." Breda took a deep breath, still watching herself in the mirror. "I think you know."

"Do I?"

"Mom, just stop. *Stop*. He's my dad. Isn't he?"

Breda had imagined all sorts of things her mom might say or do when confronted about the identity of her father. But she hadn't predicted *this*. She hadn't predicted *laughter*.

"*Mom*."

"Oh, Breda." Her mother was laughing so hard she was coughing.

"So is that a no? This isn't *funny*."

"Oh, but it *is*. Mícheál *Sullivan*? That clown? That absolute amadán? Give me *some* credit, love, will you? Where on earth did you get *that* idea?"

"Mom, *stop* laughing." Breda stepped out of the bathroom. Her head was spinning. "We met him at the pub a couple weeks ago and he was, like, *staring* at me like he knew me or something, and then Noeleen told me not to tell Granda he'd spoken to me, and then there was this woman at Inch who said I had his *eyes*, and then, just this afternoon, Tadgh Fahey took us out to the beehive huts and Nellie told me—"

"Wait." Maura's laughter had stopped as suddenly as if she'd flipped a switch. "Who?"

"The beehive huts. We went out there today."

"With Tadgh? Tadgh Fahey took you to the beehive huts?"

"Yeah. He's Nellie's uncle."

"I know that." Maura cleared her throat. "I know that. And did he drop you back at home as well? To the farm?"

"No. He took me as far as Ventry, but I didn't want Granda seeing his truck."

"Smart."

"I rode my bike the rest of the way home."

"*My* bike." Her mom's voice was quiet, as if she was speaking to herself. "The two of us, we were like Niamh and Oisín of the old legend, cycling the peninsula together. Me on my blue Raleigh and he on his red Trek. We pretended they were our horses."

"Wait." Breda sat down heavily on her bed, suddenly confused. "You and Tadgh Fahey?"

In the short silence that followed, Breda imagined her mom stretched on the couch in their little front room, a cooling cup of Barry's Tea on the end table, her long-nailed fingers wrapping around a coil of her beautiful hair.

"Yes, Breda," she said at last. "Tadgh Fahey, your father."

28.

So THERE IT WAS. BREDA HAD GONE searching down the wrong path, but she'd found her answer just the same. Her dad had a name and a face. Tadgh Fahey. He was tall and redheaded and had freckled muscular arms and wore rubber knee boots and was a veterinarian. He'd put down five sheep to save the rest of the flock from maggots and it made him angry when people didn't protect their horses from the rain. He was not a criminal or a thief, and neither was anyone else in his family. The only crime the Faheys had committed was the crime that Granda could not forgive—that one of their children had made a baby with his daughter.

"I was seventeen, Breda, and so was he," her mom explained.

"We were so young."

"And he just, what? *Dumped* you when you told him you were pregnant with me?"

"It's not that simple."

"But didn't he ever try to see you again? To get you to come back to Ireland? To come visit? To see *me*?"

"Oh, he's tried to contact me a fair bit over the years. But I was so angry with him that I never responded. I know now that he was young, too. That he was scared, too. But it seemed terribly unfair to me at the time—it still does—that a father can just walk away like that. But a mother never can. And to be clear, Breda, I never *wanted* to walk away from you. You're the best thing that's ever happened to me." On the other end of the line, her mom's voice was breaking. Breda was stunned. Maura Moriarity almost never cried. She'd been raised by Granda, after all. "I had a friend from school with an older cousin living in Chicago; she put me in touch, and that's how I met Nuala. As soon as I talked to her, Nuala promised that if I wanted to come out, she'd help me find work and give me a place to stay until you were born and I was able to get on my feet. God bless her, we ended up living with her for three years, and she never charged us a penny."

Breda cringed a little, remembering how she'd coveted that

little crystal frog on Nuala's kitchen windowsill and then pocketed it. All her earliest memory fragments took place in that kitchen—the snack drawer filled with Curly Wurly bars and Pringles, the little stand on the counter with the hook for hanging bananas, the poetry word magnets on the fridge that her mother had used to teach her how to read. How could she have done something so petty and awful?

"But even with Nuala's generosity, those first years in America, as a single mom, undocumented, so young and poor—they were very hard, Breda. I longed to go back to Ballyglass, would have gone home in a heartbeat, but I was too stubborn."

"Tadgh could have at least sent you money," Breda said. "Couldn't he have at *least* done that?"

"Well, for one thing, he wouldn't have a clue where to send it. Do you think he could have asked my father? Tadgh has enough sense to know that if he dared come anywhere *near* Davey Moriarity, your granda would knock him flat out. And anyway, I wouldn't have taken it. Taking his money might have meant he had some claim on you, some right to you, which I didn't feel that he deserved." She was quiet for a moment. "I don't know now, though. Maybe I was wrong about that. And anyway, it's not entirely Tadgh's fault. After all, it was your granda who—" She stopped. "Forget it."

"*What?*" Down the hall, Breda heard the back door open and shut. Granda had returned from the fields. She lowered her voice. "Come *on*, Mom. If you're finally gonna tell me the truth, then you've got to tell me all of it."

"Right then," her mom said quietly. "You're right, Breda. Enough with the secrets. I didn't decide to go to America when things with me and Tadgh fell apart. It was a few weeks after that, when I told your granda I was expecting you. Now, your granda is old-school, in case you haven't noticed. Tadgh and I, we weren't married, of course. And my father was furious. *Furious.* He told me to get out. Threw a bunch of euro notes at me and called me a— Well, I won't repeat what he called me."

Breda swallowed. She knew these kinds of words. She'd heard kids at school say them about her mom, just because of the way she dressed and wore her makeup.

"I'd say he thought I'd go up the road, stay with one of my friends. Which I did, until my passport arrived. Booked my flight that very day."

"Didn't he try to stop you?"

"I didn't tell him I'd gone until I'd landed in O'Hare. Rang him from Nuala's phone and told him not to bother coming after me."

"And he actually *listened*? He didn't try to come get you back?"

"He didn't. He'd say it's because he's terrified of flying. But of course I know the real reason. He was ashamed of me. He still is." She laughed bitterly. "After all, according to him, I'm a 'fallen woman.'"

Breda shook her head in disbelief. How could Granda have called his own daughter such names? How could he have thrown her out on the street when she needed him the most? How could he *still* be so angry, over a decade later, that he'd forbidden Breda from stepping foot in Fahey's Pub?

How could a man so full of wisdom be so wrong, so cold and cruel and *wrong*, when it came to his own life?

"Look, Breda. I know this is a lot to take in, yeah? But the fact is, none of it matters anymore. I'm not even angry at your granda any longer, or at Tadgh. And you shouldn't be, either. I don't feel much of anything at all toward either one of them, to tell you the truth. Because you and I, *we* are our family. *We've* built our life together from nothing, and neither your father nor your grandfather had anything to do with it. You and me, Breda. And the two of them's punishment, they missed out on your whole life. Nearly thirteen years of *you*, and they can never, ever get that back, can they?"

Breda nodded, forgetting, for a moment, that her mom couldn't see her.

"Me myself, I can't imagine a worse punishment than that."

"Thanks, Mom," she whispered. And for a moment she felt better, because Maura Moriarity never said things she didn't mean.

After they hung up, Breda lay in bed, listening to Granda bustle around the kitchen, preparing dinner for the two of them. She paged through her notebook, reading her entries about the things that had happened over the summer. The birth of Bo, her picnic with Granda on the river. The Salmon of Knowledge and the nights at An Bradán, listening to his stories. She had never expected this summer to be so wonderful, but now it was all ruined. How was she supposed to share a bowl of soup with him right now? How was she expected to live under the same roof as him for eight more weeks, now that she knew what he'd done to her mom? How could she even speak to him, let alone smile at him, respect him?

If she were to ask Granda, she was certain he would have his own version of what had happened. But she knew she would not ask. After all, he was the one who'd said that truth was a thing more slippery than a fish. He didn't believe in the truth. He only believed in his own stories. And what did

Breda believe? At least this: no matter how much she hated the taste of fish, if the Salmon of Knowledge ever appeared to her in the river waters, she would spear it through the heart and eat as much of it as her belly could hold.

29.

BREDA AND GRANDA ALWAYS ATE DINNER together at five thirty. At five forty-five that evening, she heard his heavy footsteps coming down the hallway, saw his shadow hovering on the other side of her bedroom door. But she knew that he would never actually knock and ask her to join him. And he didn't. He only stood a few minutes longer, and then she heard his steps receding back to the kitchen. For the rest of the night, she lay in bed with her door firmly shut, her stomach growling, tortured by the smells of homemade soup and brown bread wafting down the hallway. The next morning, she opened her bedroom door and felt a pang of guilt at the tray of cold soup and stale bread that he'd left outside her room. But then she reminded herself of how he'd treated her mom, and the guilt went away.

It went on like this for the rest of the week. Granda must have noticed that Breda was avoiding him, but he never bothered asking her what was wrong. She left the house every morning before he got up, ate breakfast alone, and had her lunch on the road. She made it her business never to return home from her rides until at least seven. If this made him angry, or if it hurt his feelings, he never said so. He simply took to leaving her meals on the stove, covered with a dish towel. It was never fish, but always one of her favorites—bacon and cabbage, chicken curry, chops and mashed potatoes. She ate alone at the kitchen table, washed her dishes, and went straight to bed. She never thanked him.

By the end of the week, the bad weather had returned, and Breda was glad. She could already tell the difference between the many kinds of Irish rain; this one was fierce, and would last all day. It meant she couldn't go riding, but it also meant there would be no training tonight, which saved her from coming up with an excuse to Nellie for why she wasn't going to come to Castlemaine. Maybe her mom wasn't angry at Granda or Tadgh anymore, but then, she'd had thirteen years to get over it. Breda couldn't stand the thought of facing Tadgh again, now that she knew the truth. Now that she knew that half the kids she'd been playing football with this summer were related to her. A tight clan of laughing, joking cousin-friends with history and memories and inside jokes, who'd gotten to grow up together as a family, while she'd been left behind. Who, even now, believed she was Mícheál Sullivan's daughter, and no relation to them at all.

She spent the day holed up in her bedroom, reading paper-backs and listening to the rain drum against the roof. The only time she left her room was to grab some food while Granda was out on the digger or to visit Bo in the barn. She'd been planning to spend her Friday night writing in her notebook, then going to bed early, but that evening, around seven, she heard a tenta-tive knock on her bedroom door.

"Breda? You in there, love?"

It was one thing to ignore Granda, but Noeleen was a differ-ent story. Breda got up and opened the door.

"You feeling alright, pet?" Noeleen reached out, her brow furrowed, and placed the back of her hand against Breda's fore-head. "Davey says you've been in bed all day."

"I'm fine, thanks." Breda forced a smile, ducking away from Noeleen's palm. "Just tired. And there's not much to do around here when it rains."

"Well, we're heading down to An Bradán in a bit for another

session. We would love it if you joined us."

"I don't know." Breda stood one socked foot on top of the other, biting her lip.

"Ah, go on, pet. If you don't come, I'll be sitting all alone. And what fun is that?" She glanced down the hallway, then lowered her voice. "Besides, he's been complaining that you've been 'in a mood' all week and that I shouldn't bother asking you a'tall. I told him he just doesn't know a thing about teenage girls. Help me prove him wrong?"

This time, Breda's smile was real. She didn't want to give Granda any kind of satisfaction, thinking he could predict anything about what she would or wouldn't do. Besides, if he was performing, that meant she wouldn't have to talk to him.

"Alright," she said. "Just let me get dressed."

This night, though, was quite different from the other times Breda had watched Granda transform into the seanchaí. For one thing, the weather kept the crowds away. The only audience in the quiet, dark pub was a handful of locals and a small group of intrepid German backpackers. JohnJoe, Jack, and Luke played a set of trad tunes—minor key, wordless songs, like "The Lonesome Boatman," while Granda drank a pint of Guinness, listening in silence. By the time the session was nearly over and a rainy darkness had sunk outside the windows of the pub, Breda was convinced the seanchaí wouldn't be performing at all. But then, just before the barman announced closing time, Granda adjusted the mic and began to speak.

"A long time ago," he began over the gentle minor strumming of JohnJoe's guitar, "but not so very long ago as you might think, a moss-grown stone house stood by the sea. And in this house, silent women who dressed all in black slipped through the hallways, their feet echoing on the stone.

"There were two kinds of women who lived in this house. The good women were the ones in black, and the bad women were the younger ones, the ones in thin white gowns that skimmed over their big round bellies.

"The good women in black were the helpers. They helped the bad women bear children, and as soon as the babies were born, the good women in black snatched the children away before the bad women could taint the innocent with their sin. The good women in black took the newborn babies and swaddled them up tight, then sent the bad women away, brokenhearted and empty, while they still bled and leaked milk. They told the bad women to forget, to go home and repent, for they had brought shame upon their families with those big bellies and no husbands to speak of. They said that if the bad women lived their lives from now on in faithfulness and chastity, perhaps, with the forgiveness of God, they, too, could become good women someday."

Granda paused to take a sip from his drink, and as he did so the few tourists who'd braved the rain stood uneasily and slipped out the door. This wasn't good craic, this story. This talk of bad women and leaking milk and stolen babies—it wasn't what they'd imagined when they'd come on their holidays. This wasn't a fun shivery story that you knew to be a tall tale like the fairies and the banshees. This was something else, something dark and painful and true. A glaze had come over Granda's eyes, and Breda could see that he was not in the pub anymore, not in his mind, anyway. He had left the pub to become his story.

"Many of the bad women's children were born sick and weak, and would not long survive the cold sea drafts and the loveless chill that blew through that house. When their little hearts gave out, the good women in black wound their small limp bodies in bolts of muslin and buried them, unloved and unnamed, in a wet clay garden at the edge of the sea. Over the years, the garden of lost children grew and grew, so large that the living children could not play outside without stepping on their graves. The air was thick with lost spirits, and oh, how the banshees wailed at night in that place.

"Some of the children who managed to live were adopted

into happy homes, where they were loved and reared and went on to live the normal lives of people who are born free of shame. But some of the children, the ones who cried or fussed and threw tantrums or wept for the sinful mothers that they still could feel, if not remember—they were as unwanted as their mothers had been. And so they stayed on at the stone house by the sea, reared on cold porridge and thin cabbage soup. They grew up reedy and stooped, fed with little more than silence and prayer, and leathered across the backs of their knees for the smallest infraction or evidence of insolence. They chopped wood and scrubbed laundry and washed floorboards. They could fix leaking pipes or broken furnaces. They knew all their prayers by heart—Fáilte an Aingil, Ár nAthair, the Memorare, and most of all, the Act of Contrition, which is the prayer that asks for forgiveness—but they were never taught to read or write. And so these boys and girls grew up utterly alone, friendless and wretched, until they were old enough to run away, and run away they did, in droves, as soon as they reached thirteen, to Dublin, to London, to Belfast. Nobody ever cared enough to go after them, and thus, when they ran, they were granted the poisonous freedom of those who know that they answer to no one because they are loved by no one.

"These orphans never returned to the moss-grown castle by the sea until one day, when word traveled round through the newspapers. And these unwanted children, grown now, walking past the newsstand in London or Liverpool or Cork City, saw the headline. They were still as poor as ever, but that day they splurged and bought the newspaper. They read of the frayed wire in the storeroom wall that had sparked the fire that blazed up through bags of dried oats and roared through those cold stone hallways, turning all their terrible memories to rubble. It was only then that they returned to the place where they were born. Not to pay respects, and not to remember their childhoods, but to dance, at last, upon its ashes."

Granda pushed the mic away from his face, and the applause from the small crowd was sparse. Breda got up and went to the bathroom. When she came out, Noeleen was standing at the small, rust-spotted sink, dabbing at her eye makeup.

"Noeleen?" she said. "Are you okay?"

Noeleen sniffled and dragged her fingers beneath her eyes, where her mascara had smudged.

"Sorry, love," she said. "It's just enough to break my heart, hearing that story." She looked at Breda in the mirror with shining eyes. "Y'know tis true, don't you?"

"What is?"

"Davey's story. The one he just told. He was raised in a home like that."

"I thought he was born in Kerry." Breda turned on the sink and began carefully washing her hands. "I thought he'd lived in Dingle all his life."

"Oh no, my dear. He didn't come to Dingle until he married your grandmother, God rest her. Davey's people had no land, at least none that we know of. He grew up with nothing."

"So he was an orphan?"

"Not quite. He wouldn't like that word. *Orphan.* He had a mother and he believes she would have loved him and reared him if the women in the home hadn't snatched him away from her."

Breda turned off the faucet, shook out her dripping hands. "Noeleen, I don't get it. He was—are you saying he was kidnapped?"

Noeleen sighed, and began reapplying her lipstick. "Breda, when your granda and I were growing up, Ireland was a very different place than it is now. A very . . . traditional sort of place. Old-fashioned, you might say, though of course we didn't see it that way. Your granda's mother, whoever she was, was sent to this home. By her own family. Twas a common practice back then, if a woman was expecting a child outside of marriage. A way of 'saving' her from disgrace. Twas there she gave birth to your granda, and then was sent back home again right away. Without her baby. We don't even know her name, or the name of her village. Twas the nuns who named and raised Davey. It was—now, he don't talk much about private things, you see. But I know it was very difficult for him. Very difficult, indeed. They beat him, starved him . . . things like that. They made him feel he was nothing, all because he'd been born to a mother who they believed to be a sinner."

So that was it. The story he'd just told: it wasn't the story of Ireland's history, like the Salmon of Knowledge, and it wasn't a story of Irish legend, like fairies or banshees. It was his own story, the story of his life.

"Noeleen?"

"Yes, pet?"

"Do you know about the night terrors?"

"I do, pet. I do. You understand now where they come from?" Breda nodded.

"He really never had a childhood a'tall, sure. He can be a hard man, God knows. But it's simply all those layers of scar tissue; the scars to protect his poor heart."

Noeleen reached out, suddenly, and gave Breda a tight hug.

"Be good to him, Breda. Do. He may be a hard man to love, but love is exactly what he needs. Love, to make up for a whole lifetime of never having it."

"I'll try," Breda said, her voice muffled in the perfumed wool of Noeleen's cardigan. "I promise."

But loving him could be so hard.

Because the next morning, when Breda awoke and looked out the window, she saw that Granda had turned Bo out to pasture. The little creature stood cowering beneath his mother's legs, his brown fur turning matted and black in the downpour. Breda stood watching, lit up with anger. When his own daughter had come to him and told him a baby was coming, he could have held her, helped her, been happy for her. Instead he'd turned his back on her. It was not his fault that he'd lost his own mother. But he had no one to blame but himself for losing his daughter, too. *If only you listen, there are many things that I can teach you*, he'd said, and Breda had believed him. But what could he teach her? The names of flowers and trees? The silly stories of fairies and swan-children and genius fish? When it came to the things that really mattered, when it came to *life*, that's where he came up empty. He was a bitter old man, and he had learned nothing.

30.

THIS WAS HOW JULY CONTINUED BETWEEN Breda and Granda, plodding and bitter. And then, one glorious afternoon filled with light and tumbling clouds, Breda stopped at the little pub in Inch for her Smoky Bacon Taytos and blackcurrant. She was sitting at her favorite picnic table, eavesdropping on the tourists, when a tall shadow fell across her table. Breda looked up. Tadgh Fahey stood before her, looking as nervous as some of the shyer boys in school before getting up to give a presentation. Now that he was standing this close to her, close enough to touch, her father, she felt an ache, a fluttering in her stomach. She couldn't tell if it was nerves or anger.

"Hiya, Breda," he said, kneading his fingers together and looking at the ground. "I'm—sorry to interrupt. But tis been bothering me for days now and here you are so I s'posed I'd ask you. When I was helping you with your bicycle the other day. . . I swear it looked just like the one a girl I used to—em."

"It *is* the same one," Breda said quietly.

"Em—sorry?"

"You and Maura. Pretending you were Niamh and Oisín. My granda is Davey Moriarity. I'm staying with him for the summer. He gave me that bike. It used to be my mother's."

She watched his Adam's apple jump as the meaning sank in. The next table over, two French girls were arguing about something, but in their language it sounded musical.

"Maura Moriarity is your—*mother?*"

She nodded.

"So that means . . . so that means . . ." He trailed off.

"Yes. That's what it means." She grabbed her half-eaten bag of Taytos and stood up.

"Wait." He reached out a hand, but Breda backed away. "Please, Breda. I—I know it's a lot to ask. But if I could explain it to you. If you could let me explain. Please, I—"

"No." Her heart was pounding wildly. It felt like the sun was flooding her eyes, like she couldn't see. She felt tears brimming. Why? He was just a stranger. Like her mom said, she didn't care about him either way, not anymore. It had been too long. But still—

"Let me take you out. One lunch. Even if you never want to see me again after that, it would be lovely just to share a meal with my daughter."

At those two words, Breda froze. *My daughter.* Tadgh Fahey was her father: this she knew. But she hadn't yet considered the other side of that same coin: that she was Tadgh Fahey's daughter.

"Please, Breda. One meal. And I'll never be a bother to you again, unless you want me to be."

Breda stared at him, thinking. It might be worth it, just to be able to tell her mom about it. Just to be able, after all these years, to deliver Maura the apology she deserved. Her mother could never return to Ireland; her life, however undocumented, was in America now. In the US, there would always be people— people like Breda's teacher, Ms. Landry—who would despise her mom and call her "illegal alien," but as the years went by, her mother's memories of home would eventually begin to fade right along with her accent. She belonged nowhere, to no country. If Tadgh wanted to say he was sorry for helping to cause that, he could say it to Breda's face. It was the next best thing.

"Fine," she said, stuffing her bag of chips into her pocket and walking toward her bike. "One meal and that's it."

31.

WHAT DO YOU WEAR TO A LUNCH WITH the father you've just met? Do you dress up, to show him how well you've done without him? Do you dress down, to show him you don't care? Do you put on some makeup, so he knows how grown you are, nearly a teenager by the time he first saw your face? Or do you go without even a swipe of mascara, so that he can better see that face, a face he gave you and one that he'll never see again?

In the end, Breda realized there was no point in overthinking it. She wore her usual: tank top, athletic shorts, ponytail. If Tadgh didn't like it, too bad. She didn't care what he thought anyway.

When Tadgh had suggested they meet for lunch at Fahey's

Pub, Breda balked for a moment before she remembered that she no longer cared for Granda's rules. She would go where she wanted, when she wanted, and there was nothing he could do to stop her.

That afternoon, Tadgh was waiting at a table near the window, and stood up as she approached him. She was afraid he would try to hug her—what would it feel like to be hugged by her father?—so she slid into the booth quickly, before he got the chance. When he sat down across from her, she could see two spots of color on his cheeks. It made her feel a little bit better to see that he was just as nervous as she was—maybe even more, because after all, *she* wasn't the one who'd been a huge jerk all these years.

"Breda," he said. "I'm so glad you came. I thought you might stand me up."

"When I say I'll be somewhere, I'll be somewhere," she said, trying to channel her mother's toughness. "It's called personal accountability. Ever heard of it?"

"I have," he said quietly. "You look just like her. You've got her fire, too."

Breda looked down at the scuffed wooden table, unable to think of how to respond to this.

"How is she, anyway?"

"Fine."

"You know, I always thought she'd come back home." He put his hands around his pint of water. "I s'pose she never will, at this stage."

"She couldn't even if she wanted to. She's undocumented. If she tried to come for a visit, she would never be allowed back into the States."

"Doesn't seem right to me that a Kerrywoman could never come home to Kerry."

"Kerry isn't her home, not anymore. We're Americans. She owns her own business. Did you know that?"

"I didn't." He drank his water. "But she was always the smartest girl in the room, so she was. What kind of business is it?"

"She owns a hair salon."

Nellie arrived now, holding a plate in each hand.

"Hey, cuz," she said, and winked. "Now we'll defo do that J-1 summer, yeah?"

Breda smiled weakly.

"Enjoy your chat, anyway." She placed a toasted sandwich and salad in front of Breda and an identical one in front of Tadgh, then walked away. Neither one of them made any motion to start eating.

"I'm sorry, Breda. I am. It's just— I have a daughter, like. A beautiful daughter, sitting right before me. I'm totally gobsmacked."

"My mother has a daughter. You don't have anything."

He cast his eyes down at his untouched food.

"Everything she has, she's had to work for," Breda said, her voice shaking. "With no help from anyone. No family. When you're undocumented, you're so alone, do you get that? Nobody helps you. Nobody feels sorry for you. Nobody wants you around. And still, *still*, she succeeded. Do you get that? Do you get how freaking *cool* that is?"

"I do. I *do*."

"You could have helped her. I'm sure you make plenty of money. But you didn't."

"I wasn't always a vet," he said softly. "And I certainly didn't always have money. Not that I'm making excuses, now."

"Well, I guess it's fine, because she didn't need you, anyway."

"Breda, there are so many things I would do differently if I only could. So many." He tried to touch her hand but she pulled it away. She thought of all those years when her mom had worked and worked and still there was no money. How she was always so tired. And that day at Sophie Taylor's birthday party, the moment when Breda understood that the other kids at school would never accept her, because their parents didn't accept her mother. That maybe there was even a parent among the ones at that party, drinking coffee and gossiping, who might, if they ever found out the truth about Maura's status, report her themselves.

"But you *can't* change anything," Breda said softly, and even though she was furious at herself, she was crying now. "That's the thing. You can ask for forgiveness, but you can never go back and fix what's already been done."

Tadgh's eyes were now filled with tears, too. "But that's why I'm here, Breda. To ask for your forgiveness. And your mother's. To see if there's any way—if I could be in your life now. Maybe Maura can't come home, but I could come to Chicago, for a visit."

"I don't know." Breda stared at the toasted surface of her sandwich and wiped her eyes. The fact that he was almost crying too made everything feel worse. "I'd have to ask her. She works a lot. And I don't know if she'd even want to see you."

The rest of the meal was awkward and mostly silent. They both picked at their food, and when they were finished and Tadgh paid the bill, he insisted on walking her outside to her bike.

"You sure I can't give you a lift home?"

She shook her head.

"Right then." He reached into his pocket and dug out an old Tesco receipt and a stubby carpenter's pencil. "Let me at least give you my mobile number. If you ever want to speak more—that would be lovely." She watched him write down the number and tried not to notice how he wrote his *4*'s the same way she did. "And if you ever need anything at all, don't hesitate to ring."

"Alright." She took the receipt from him and stuffed it into her pocket.

"Well, then. I s'pose this is goodbye, so."

"I guess it is."

They stood there for a moment on the sidewalk outside the pub. Breda felt a softening in her heart, just for a moment. The way he stood there, a grown-up man who looked as sorry as a sick cow. She opened her mouth to say to him—*I'll talk to my mom. Maybe you can come, if you stay in a hotel. Maybe we could all go to lunch together*—but before she could, a familiar blue Opel passed by on the quiet street. It slowed down but did not stop as it passed them by. And before it drove on, Noeleen locked eyes with Breda, and it was too late now to stop what was to come.

32.

FOR THREE DAYS, NOTHING HAPPENED. Breda continued to avoid Granda. She refused to feel any regret for going to lunch with Tadgh. If Noeleen decided to tell Granda what she'd seen, who cared? Everyone in this family lived their lives hiding in a cloud of secrets; they couldn't decide to get angry when she did the same. Still, every time she thought about it, about Granda knowing what she'd been up to and who she'd been hanging around with this summer, she felt a plume of dread uncurling in her stomach.

And then, in the middle of a clear, cool night, a crying sound awoke Breda from a dead sleep. She sat up in bed, holding her breath, listening. And then the scream came again. Like last time, she could tell that it wasn't coming from Granda's bedroom. It was coming from outside her window. She braced herself before she pulled back her curtains, expecting to see the specter of a banshee leaning against the stone fence. But all that was there was the dark shape of one of Granda's cows in the pasture. The creature was standing alone near the fence, bellowing again and again. It was clear that something was wrong, but what could it be? Breda slipped out of bed, snuck past Granda's closed bedroom door, pulled on her wellies, and went outside to investigate.

Outside, when she walked right up to the fence, the cow wouldn't even look at her. It was staring off toward the big barn, bellowing. Now that she was closer, Breda recognized the diamond-shaped brown spot between its eyes. It was Bo's mother. She wasn't bleeding or limping, but it was clear that something was terribly wrong.

Breda went back inside and knocked softly on Granda's bedroom door. She wasn't exactly thrilled at the idea of speaking to him, but what if something really bad was happening? What if the cow had some sort of illness, some disease that could spread to the other cows and kill the whole herd? Since he certainly wouldn't ever call Tadgh Fahey for veterinary help, would Granda end up destitute, like the sheep farmer who'd been visited by the banshee? Her mother had sent her to Ireland so that she could learn how to be a better person, to take responsibility, and this was her, doing that. Being mature. Gently, she pushed open the door.

"Granda?"

He was asleep on his back, his mouth hanging open. Without his false teeth in, his lips caved together, and in his thin yellow nightshirt with the blankets pulled up to his chest, he looked so defenseless. For a moment, she pitied him. She said his name again. This time he shot up with a shout, and for a moment the look in his blue eyes flashing in the starlight was pure terror.

"Granda, it's just me."

"What in the name of God?" He passed a hand over his face and looked up at her.

"Granda, something's wrong with one of the cows."

He stared at her, his eyes slowly coming into focus.

"It's Bo's mother. She's—like, wailing. And pacing up and down alone in the pasture. I think she's hurt."

"Jaysus, Breda." He slumped back against his wooden head-board. "You frightened the life out of me."

"But what about the cow?"

"The cow's grand. Go back to bed now."

"She's not! She's going crazy out there! Don't you hear that?"

Breda stood there at the edge of his bed and the two of them were silent, listening to Bo's mother's frantic bellowing.

"Sure you'd have to be deaf not to hear that carry-on."

"Well, can't you *do* something? Check on her at least, to make sure she's not hurt?"

"Breda, she's grand. She'll wear herself out, so she will. In a few days she'll be perfectly well."

"But what's *wrong* with her?"

"She's just missing her baby, is all."

"What? What do you mean? Did something happen to Bo?"

Granda sighed, leaned over, and clicked on his bedside lamp. "Sure I sold the little fella at the cattle mart this morning."

Breda stared at him. "You—you *sold* Bo?"

"Sure he's going to make a grand bull one day."

"How could you *sell* him? He's a *baby*!"

"Ah, he was a biteen young to take from his mother, but sure there was a buyer who was willing to pay a good price, and sometimes you have to take the opportunities that come your way."

Breda stood there, gaping at him. The cruelty of it. Bo was just a baby. Who would feed him? Who would care for him? Tears gathered and spilled down her face as she imagined that sweet calf, with his soft fur and dark eyes, whose birth she had helped make possible, being prodded up the metal ramp on the way to slaughter.

"Ah, Breda," he said, rolling his eyes. "This is why I told you: they're livestock. You shouldn't ever name them. You mustn't think of them as animals, even. You think of them as money on four legs. Tisn't a charity I'm running here."

He pulled the covers up and rolled over to the side, turning his back to her.

"You could have at least told me before you did it."

"Why? It wouldn't have changed the outcome."

"I'm counting down the days for summer to be over, so I never have to see you again." She said the words quietly to the back of his silver head, hating him. "You're nothing but a pathetic old man."

At that, he turned slowly to face her. His face in the lamplight was as fierce and craggy as the cliffs in Castlemaine Harbour. "I asked you *one* thing for the whole of this summer," he said, his voice low, almost dangerous. "*One*. And you disobeyed me. It'll be all the village is talking about for months. Davey's granddaughter went behind his back, broke bread with his enemy."

"So Noeleen told you."

"She did of course, and don't waste your time being angry with her because if she hadn't, t'would have been someone else who told me. You know nothing about village life, girl."

"You did this on purpose. You *sold Bo* just to get back at me."

"I s'pose you know what that man did to your mother. First disgraced her, then abandoned her. Forced her from Ballyglass—from her home, her *real* home—forever."

"She's not disgraced! She's a successful businesswoman, and she moved away from home not because of Tadgh but because of *you*."

He waved her off. "Go to bed now, and let me be."

"Listen to that mother out there! She may only be 'livestock,' but guess what, Granda? She loves her baby more than you ever loved yours!"

"You know nothing about life, child!" he shouted. "And you're soft in the head to care so much about a bloody cow! Now, for the last time, get yourself to bed!"

"I hate you!"

"Grand, so! Hate me all you like!"

She ran down the hall to her bedroom, slammed the door so hard the house shook, and threw herself down on the bed. This was the worst part of being a kid: this feeling of being trapped. She wanted to leave, to run away, but there was nowhere to go and even if there was, there was no way of getting there. Instead she must lie here all night, beneath the roof of a man she hated, unable to stopper her ears from the sounds just outside her window, the anguished sounds of a mother whose baby had been taken away from her.

Hurry up, sunrise, she wrote furiously in her journal. As soon as you show up, I'm gone.

33.

AS IT TURNED OUT, IT WAS ACTUALLY before sunrise when Jake came running into Breda's room, yipping and whining, his claws scrabbling across the hardwood.

"Jake?" She sat up in bed and rubbed her eyes. The sky outside her window was awash in a rainbow of dark purples. "What are you doing in here, buddy?" She reached down to rub the top of his head, but he scrambled away, running back and forth next to her bed and continuing to whine.

"Jake, what *is* it?"

With a quick movement, the dog leaped onto her bed. He smelled of grass and the outdoors, and he was leaving muddy paw prints all over her comforter.

"Jake! Naughty! You know you're not allowed on the furnit—"

He began to howl now, and nudge her with his wet nose, trying to push her out of bed. She'd never seen him behave this way before. Breda threw back her covers.

"Jake, what's the *matter?*"

He hopped down from her bed and began spinning in frantic circles at her doorway, as if to tell her to hurry up and follow him. As soon as she stood up, he sprinted down the long hallway, barking and whining. She had to break into a run to catch up.

When she reached the kitchen, Breda froze. Granda always closed and locked the door before bed each night, but here it stood wide open as a screaming mouth, ready to welcome whatever strange creature, banshee or human, who might care to stroll inside.

It was now that she began to feel afraid.

Jake whined again, and nudged Breda's wellies toward her. As soon as she'd pulled them on, he bolted outside in the direction of the great green hill.

The sun was beginning to come up, and the fog that hung over the driveway was suffused with golden light. As she followed him through the mist and up the hill, Jake's little white figure kept disappearing, then reappearing, in the hanging shroud of wispy white, like an apparition. Breda shivered, jogging to keep up. She thought of Granda's stories about the fairies, those evil and cruel creatures who were as far from sweet little Disney Tinker Bells as could be, and of how they could shape-shift. Of how they often took the forms of dogs. She had to remind herself to be reasonable: Granda's stories were just that, stories, and there was no reason to be afraid. Dogs sometimes got notions in their heads, just like people did. Jake was just Jake, and she needed to calm down.

They were about halfway up the hill when the fog began to dissipate. Following Jake, Breda could make various shapes out of the disappearing mist: the trunks of aspen, the delicate waving petals of maidenhair. And then, stony and still like the great unmoving Blasket Islands, a large shape in the grass. A shape that looked out of place.

A human shape.

Jake sprinted toward it at full speed, and when he began to howl again, Breda finally realized what it was she was running toward.

34.

HE WAS LYING FACEDOWN IN THE GRASS.
His yellow nightshirt, wet with dew, clung to the knobs of his spine.

"Granda?"

She put her hand gingerly on his thick, muscled shoulder. His pajama top was cold and wet. With some effort, she turned him gently to the side—the blue of his eyes was hidden behind the thin closed skin of his lids, and his mouth hung open, a black hole without his false teeth to fill them. A sour smell was coming off his skin. Breda took a deep breath and placed two of her fingers on his cold neck, the way they'd been taught to do in health class. At first she felt nothing, but then she found it, and her insides went liquidy with relief—a faint but steady pulse. He was alive.

"Jake," she said, her voice breaking, "what was he *doing* out here?"

The little white dog stared at her and began to whine again. She'd forgotten, for just a second, that he couldn't answer her.

"Wait here, buddy," she commanded. "I'm going to get help."

As she ran the rest of the way down the hill and toward the house, Breda considered what to do. Granda had told her, on her first day at the farm, the number for emergency services. It was not 911, like in America. It was something else. But for the life of her she couldn't remember what it was. 311? 099? 353? No, that was the country code. She couldn't remember. The Fianna could run through the forest without snapping a twig, and she couldn't remember a phone number. Who else could she call? Noeleen, of course, but she didn't have Noeleen's number, either. The fact was, she only had one phone number in the whole of the Dingle Peninsula. *If you ever need anything at all*, he'd told her, *don't hesitate to ring*.

She knew that if Granda were conscious, he would tell her, *I'd rather die than accept help from that man.* Except it wasn't his choice anymore. Because Breda needed him, desperately, to

202

live. As rocky as their summer had been, he was still her blood. He was hers.

She went into her bedroom and unfolded the Tesco receipt Tadgh Fahey had given her. She took a breath and dialed the numbers. He answered on the very first ring.

35.

TADGH'S VAN CAME BARRELING UP THE driveway, the tires spraying gravel, and screeched to a stop next to the clothesline. Breda ran out to meet him.

"Breda." He climbed out of the truck and hesitated, as if reminding himself not to try to hug her. "I'm so glad you rang."

"I had no one else to call."

He winced a little at that, but it was the truth, and she didn't want him confusing the need for help with a desire for a relationship.

"Where is he?"

"I'll bring you to him." She led him past the shed and toward the base of the hill. "He made it halfway to the top."

"The old codger. What in the name of God was he trying to do, climbing up the hill at his age?"

"I have no idea. He must have snuck off in the middle of the night. And he knows he's not supposed to climb that hill anymore. He has a stent in his heart."

"I see," Tadgh said quietly.

They were passing the bird cherry tree now. Breda tried not to think about that day at the river, how Granda taught her that peasants once believed the tree's bark could ward off the plague. For all his faults and failings, there was still so much more she needed to learn from him. What if he died now, before she got the chance?

As they approached Granda lying motionless in the grass, Jake began to bark and growl, as if Granda had been so thorough in his anger he'd even trained his dog to hate the Faheys.

"It's okay, Jakey," Breda said, putting a hand on the dog's furry head. "He's here to help." Jake obeyed and planted himself next to her, but continued to growl low in his throat as Tadgh squatted down before Granda.

"I already checked his pulse." Breda watched him place his fingers against Granda's neck.

"Well, tis still there," Tadgh said grimly. "That's the good news. I'm going to examine him now for any external injuries."

With his expert veterinarian's hands, he began to methodically check Granda's body. First he gently examined Granda's silver head, then his neck, arms, and back. Then, very gently, he lifted up Granda's nightshirt. The skin of his abdomen was waxy and white, an entirely different color than the leathered tan of his face, as if it belonged to the body of a different, and much older, person. Breda looked away. And then, as Tadgh's hands moved down toward Granda's hips, the old man's eyelids fluttered and he groaned weakly.

"What?" Breda demanded. "What is it?"

"I believe he may have broken a major bone, love. His hip. Or maybe his pelvis." Tadgh sat back in the grass and rubbed a hand over his face. "If that's it, Breda—well, tis a very serious injury. Especially for a man of his age. If it's the pelvis, then this is very serious indeed."

Breda was shaking all over. She grabbed Granda's limp hand. It was clammy and puffy. The purple of his fingers was vivid against the bloodless white of the rest of his hand.

"We need to get him to a hospital straightaway." Tadgh pulled his phone from his pocket.

"Who are you calling?"

"My brothers. I need some men to help me lift him."

"But—"

"Breda, these old grudges, they need to be left in the past where they belong. If we don't get him help right away, he'll die."

Breda swallowed and nodded. She didn't want to admit it, but she knew that Tadgh was right. And that was how Granda, unconscious and cold, was carried down the hill and into the van of his sworn enemies, the Faheys.

36.

AT TRALEE GENERAL, A PACK OF MEDI-cal staff whisked Granda away through a security door. A short while later, a nurse came out to tell them he'd been moved to emergency surgery. Before Breda could ask any details, the nurse hurried off again, and she was left alone with Tadgh and his brothers in a chilly, antiseptic room where miserable-looking people limped around or held ice packs to their injuries and waited.

"We have to call Noeleen," Breda said. "She should be here for this."

"I'll track down her mobile number." Tadgh began scrolling through his phone. "We've got to know some of the same people."

"And I have to call my mom, too."

"You do of course," said Tadgh, his face reddening at even the mention of Maura. His brothers, meanwhile—who, Breda just realized, were also her uncles—stood there staring at her.

"He'll pull through," said the one with the faded red hair who she recognized as Nellie's dad. "Just a bad fall, I'd reckon."

"He will," said the other, nodding.

"I'll get you some tea," said Nellie's dad. He got up, and the other brother, clearly terrified to be alone with Breda, hurried to follow him.

Half an hour later, Noeleen came bursting through the doors of the ER, a whirlwind of lavender perfume and fretfulness. The Fahey brothers stood up, but she hurried right past them without so much as a glance and wrapped Breda in a tight hug.

"Noeleen," Breda said, taking a deep breath and giving her father a small smile, "this is Tadgh Fahey and these are his brothers. They helped me get Granda to the hospital."

"Yes, we spoke on the phone." Noeleen nodded curtly, her face revealing nothing. She turned back to Breda.

"How's our man?" she whispered.

"He's in surgery. We don't know anything more yet."

Noeleen squeezed her shoulder gently. "I'll see what I can find out." She put her purse down on an empty chair and faced the Fahey brothers. "Lads, thanks very much for your help today."

"No bother," the brothers all said to the floor.

"I'll take it from here, then."

"If tis grand with you," Tadgh said quietly, "I'd like to stay here until we hear a bit of news."

"Oh, I don't think so." Noeleen's voice was firm. "Davey wouldn't like that, and we're going to respect his wishes."

"Noeleen, it's okay," Breda said. "He can stay if he wants."

Noeleen shot Breda a look but said nothing.

"I s'pose I'll stay for a bit longer, then," Tadgh said, still looking at the floor. "I'll drop these two in town and then I'll be right back, okay, Breda?"

"Okay."

"Sure we'll be pulling for him," Nellie's dad said, and his other brother nodded in agreement.

"We appreciate it," Noeleen said coldly. She watched the three brothers walk slowly out the swinging double doors, then sat heavily in a chair.

"What I can't figure," she said, "is what in the name of God he was doing trying to climb that hill. Years ago, he used to go up the hill whenever something was troubling him. The silly man, he really believes the Salmon of Knowledge lives in his river. He'd go up there from time to time, asking for guidance, for help. I'd tell him, that's blasphemy, Davey, but do you think he cared?"

She shook her head, dug her rosary out of her purse, and began to pray the first decade, the ticking beads and her whispered Hail Marys the only sound in the now-empty waiting room. Breda watched her for a while before summoning the courage to speak.

"Noeleen?"

"Yes, pet?"

"Why did you tell Granda that I was having lunch with Tadgh?"

The older woman dropped her rosary gently in her lap.

"Sure I can't have those kinds of secrets with Davey," she said. "The man *hates* secrets. His whole childhood was filled with them. Please don't be cross with me, love. I did what I thought was right."

"I'm not." Breda cleared her throat. It had been awhile since she'd had anything to drink, and her mouth felt sour and dry. "The thing is, we had a big fight last night and—we both said some awful things. *I* said some awful things." Breda was quiet for a moment. "I think . . . I think maybe he tried to climb the hill to get answers for what to do about me. The last thing I said to him was that I hated him."

"Ah, pet."

Breda began to cry, and Noeleen wrapped her arm around her shoulder. Tadgh returned a short while later with snacks and tea, and they sat in the waiting room, eating without talking. An hour passed, then another, and another. At last, a doctor came through the swinging doors and walked toward them.

"Ms. Murphy?" he said, looking at Noeleen.

"Yes." She and Breda both leaped to their feet. They approached the doctor, with Tadgh following at a respectful distance behind them.

"I'm Dr. Philbin. I'm an orthopedic surgeon here at the hospital."

"How is he?" Breda's voice was shaking so hard she could barely get the words out. The doctor's face was grim.

"Well, I'm afraid Mr. Moriarity has broken his pelvis," he said, removing his glasses and rubbing them on his white jacket. "The break itself was fairly clean. Unfortunately—and with this kind of injury tis fairly common—there was quite a bit of internal bleeding that collected in the pelvic cavity, as well as some damage to the surrounding organs . . ."

His voice faded out for a moment, and Breda saw black spots dancing across her vision. Without realizing she was doing it, she leaned back against Tadgh and he wrapped his arms around her tightly.

". . . first surgery we were able to successfully stop the bleeding."

"That's good, then, Doctor, isn't it?" Noeleen asked in a

small voice. She still clung to her rosary beads.

"Tis a positive sign, yes. However, he will be needing a second surgery in a few days to repair the break itself. We'll use a combination of compression screws and pins—fairly straightforward, but—well. Let me be clear. With his age, and his existing health conditions, it will be difficult. The next twenty-four hours are critical. We just don't know how his body will respond."

"What are his chances?" asked Tadgh, and Breda was flooded with gratefulness that Tadgh had stayed. He was brave enough to ask the question that she herself, and even Noeleen, dared not ask.

"Well, again. There's his age. There's his other medical issues—he's a stent in his heart, and he's on blood thinners, which most likely exacerbated the bleeding," the doctor said. "If he makes it through tonight, I'd give him about a thirty percent chance. We'll know much more in the next twenty-four hours."

If? Breda thought. *If?*

"God bless you, Doctor," Noeleen said, grabbing his hand and squeezing it between both of hers while the doctor stood there looking uncomfortable. "God bless you."

"We'll keep you updated," Dr. Philbin said. "In the meantime, would you like to go see him?"

Tadgh stayed back in the waiting room while Noeleen and Breda followed the doctor down a long hallway. In his bed, Breda could barely recognize him. The tough, muscled farmer was gone, replaced by a pale old man clinging to life with the help of several beeping, whirring machines. An oxygen mask covered his mouth and nose, and all sorts of IVs sprouted from the veins in the tops of his workman's hands and the crooks of his elbows. The doctor's words—*thirty percent, if he makes it through the night*—now felt real. The sound of the banshee was drowned out by all the medical machinery, but Breda could feel it anyway—death, an old woman spirit, lurking unseen, in the corners of the room.

"Oh, Davey," Noeleen whispered, bending down to kiss him on a white-whiskered cheek. "Oh, Davey, look what's happened to you."

"Noeleen?" Breda said quietly. "Can I borrow your phone?"

37.

"**M**OM?"

"Breda!" Maura answered groggily on the last ring before voice mail. "Did you forget about the time difference? It's five in the bleeding morning here."

"Mom." Her voice broke.

"What's—" She was wide awake now. "Hush, pet. Tell me what happened."

"It's Granda," she heaved.

"What's the matter? What happened?"

"He fell, Mom. He was climbing the hill and he—"

"What was he doing climbing that blasted hill at his age? He's always been like that, thinking he's younger and tougher than he really is!"

"Mom, listen. He broke his pelvis. The doctor said something about internal bleeding and organ damage and—"

"Jesus, Mary, and Joseph. Did you say *organ*—"

"They did surgery and they managed to stop the bleeding but they said the next twenty-four hours are critical and there's only a thirty percent chance that he won't, like . . ."

Die. She couldn't say it. She heard her mother exhale a long breath.

"Mom, I think—I know it's complicated and everything, but I think you need to get on a plane. Right now. You need to come here. He needs you. *I* need you. Please. I don't think he . . . if something happens and he doesn't make it. I mean, there's a seventy percent chance he *won't* make it. And if he—if he—well, then you'll never see him again."

There was a long pause. Breda imagined her beautiful mother sitting up in bed, her hair in a messy bun, dressed in the satin cheetah-print pajamas Breda had gotten her that Christmas, which she wore almost every night.

"Breda," her mom finally said. "Love."

"Please tell me you'll come."

"Darling. You know that I can't."

"*What?* But, Mom—"

"You know what will happen if I go back to Ireland. I might be able to get a new passport from the Irish consulate—though

216

it would take weeks—but even if I could, then what? What would happen when we tried to come back to Chicago? What will I show them at customs? My visa that's been useless for nearly thirteen years?"

"It's better than nothing! It might—"

"The penalty for overstaying a ninety-day visa by even *one day* is a ten-year ban. What d'you think they'd do to a woman who overstayed for over a decade? A lifetime ban, that's what. I could never, ever come back to the US, and our whole life is here now, darling. You need to understand that. Our whole business, our whole livelihood. We've worked together as a team to build our life, and if I go back to Ireland now—for any reason, even *this*—it's all gone. Wiped away."

"But, Mom. He's your *dad*. This might be your last chance to ever see him again. To make things right."

"I know." Maura's voice was trembling. "I always knew, in the back of my mind, that this day would come. I just was in denial, I guess. Please tell him— Well, wait now. Are you there now? In the hospital?"

"Yeah, I'm in the hallway outside his room."

"Put me on with him, so."

"He's unconscious, Mom." Her voice wobbled over the word. "He's hooked up to a bunch of machines. He can't talk to you."

"Well, he can listen. For once in his life, by God, he can listen."

Breda did what she was told. She entered the room and closed the door softly behind her. Noeleen sat on one side of Granda, holding his hand and praying through her beads with her free hand. Breda walked over and held the phone up to Granda's withered ear. She could hear the murmured cadence of her mother's voice, but couldn't make out the things she was saying to him. All Breda knew was that it went on for a very long time, and that when she finally took the phone back, her mother had already hung up.

38.

THE NIGHT WAS LONG AND MOSTLY SLEEP-
less. Noeleen prayed her rosary, again and again, and
the chant of it lulled Breda into a few short naps, but mostly she
stayed awake, watching him. Her mother had raised her without religion—*Heaven? Hell? Angels? Fairy tales like that are for
wee babies. I won't coddle you*—and so Noeleen's rosary meant
nothing to her. Instead, she prayed silently to Granda himself:
Please don't die, she thought, watching his still body in the darkness. *You can't die. If you do me this one favor and don't die, I'll
forgive you for what you did to Bo and I'll forgive you for what you
did to my mom. I'll forgive you everything, if only you don't die.
Because, Granda, there's no way to fix this. Mom can't come to you.*

If you die, you'll never see her again. But if you don't die, maybe we could work something out. Maybe we could get her a visa somehow. Maybe we could slip her back in through US Customs. They don't catch everyone, do they? There's no way. Maybe there's a chance she could come home and see you. But how will we ever know, unless you do me this one favor and don't die?

She prayed to the Salmon of Knowledge, too. But there wasn't much use. The questions she had for the Salmon were unsolvable. What was the right thing for her mother to do? To give up everything she'd ever worked for to be by her father's side as he was dying? Why did the world make you choose? Why was there such a thing as an illegal person? Traffic violations could be illegal, and so could drugs and weapons, things that killed. But how could people? Even if Breda were to touch her blistered thumb to her lips and gain all the knowledge of the world, this still would be a problem without a solution. Until people stopped being illegal, it always would.

At some point, she fell into a real sleep, and sometime later, she jolted awake in her chair. Outside, the dawn was breaking and a nurse was hovering over Granda's blood pressure cuff. His heartbeat moved across the monitor without stopping, like the tide. He had made it through the night.

A new doctor arrived to examine him.

"He's very fragile," the doctor said. "What I'd like to do is to keep him sedated for now, let him rest and gain strength. If he continues to improve, we can schedule a surgery to repair his pelvis in a few days. But for now, I'm afraid I can't promise anything else." The doctor looked back and forth between Breda and Noeleen, whose eyes were red and puffy with sleeplessness.

"What I'd do now if I was the pair of you," she went on, "is let him rest and get home and rest yourselves. Come back later this afternoon when we might have a bit more news."

"Are you absolutely wrecked?" Noeleen asked as they walked through the parking lot in the soft rain.

"I'm okay." Breda yawned.

"Tell the truth, now. If you're wrecked, I can take you back to the farm and you can sleep for a bit. But if you've still got a bit of energy, would you like to go for a drive with me?"

"A drive?" Breda rubbed her eyes. "Where to?"

"You'll see, love."

Breda shrugged. "Okay."

She assumed that wherever they were going would be a quick drive somewhere on the peninsula, to get Granda some balloons, maybe an *Irish Farmers Journal* to read to him as he lay there unconscious and sedated, but instead, Noeleen's little Opel headed north on the N69 toward Listowel, in the opposite direction of Ballyglass.

Eventually, when they came back into sight of the Atlantic, Noeleen turned down a road leading to the water. Before them appeared a giant boat with a long steel ramp, and Noeleen slowed down at the entrance. Two men in orange vests were directing cars, and when they waved at Noeleen, she steered the Opel up the ramp and onto the enormous boat.

"The Tarbert Ferry," she explained, parking the car in a line with the other vehicles as if this was the most normal thing in the world. "Quickest way to get to Clare."

"Um." Breda looked out the car window at the land receding behind her. It was the strangest feeling, moving across a bay in a car that wasn't moving at all. She felt, weirdly, seasick. "What's in County Clare? What about—"

Noeleen dug out a bag of chocolate Smarties from her purse and handed some to Breda.

"Like I said, love," she said, dumping a handful into her own mouth, "you will see."

39.

IT WAS A SHORT JOURNEY ACROSS THE
Shannon Estuary, and they sat together in the parked car
atop the ferry, passing the Smarties back and forth, each lost in
their own fears for Granda. Soon enough, they arrived at the
port in Killimer, on the other side of the bay. The steel ramp
creaked down, and just like that, they were on the road again
through County Clare. After another hour or so, Breda began
to feel anxious. They were moving farther and farther away
from Granda—what if the hospital called and needed them
back right away? What if he took a turn? What if he died alone?

"Noeleen," she said, exasperated, "where are we *going*?"

"We're nearly there, love," she said. "I promise you."

They continued along the coast, and as they came around the bend, Liscannor Bay spread out before them to the west, gray and wide and beautiful. A short while later, Noeleen pulled off down a narrow side road, overgrown with trees and brush, that would easily be missed if you didn't know it was there. The trees on either side of them were so thick that branches scraped both sides of the little blue car as they drove along. And then the brush fell away and they were out in the open again. There, standing in a clearing before the foggy sea, was an enormous stone building, blackened and crumbling, with ivy curling out of the glassless windows. Noeleen got out first, and Breda followed her cautiously. There was a badness here; she could feel it as surely as if Granda had conjured it in one of his stories.

"Noeleen?" Breda said quietly. "This is the place, isn't it?"

The older woman nodded. "Come," she said, "and let me show you something."

She led Breda to a place near the edge of the water where a large, smooth rock stood in the clay. A small plaque made in bronze that was calcifying green from the constant salty wind was screwed to its surface. On the plaque was a picture of the Blessed Virgin Mary just like the one that hung over Breda's bed. *For the lost children of Saint Anthony's Home*, it read. *May they rest in peace*. Breda shivered, remembering the seanchaí's story. The babies wrapped in white muslin and buried in the clay.

"Ever notice how the man eats?" Noeleen stared at the plaque. "Stuffing the food in his mouth as quick as he can swallow?"

Breda nodded. One of the first things she'd noticed, that first day in Ballyglass when she'd shared tea with him, was how he wolfed down one Jaffa cake after another, crumbs flying from his mouth. It had disgusted her.

"When I first met him I thought twas simply bad table manners. Now I know tis because the man was barely fed a proper meal his whole boyhood. Even now, he eats like someone who's convinced there will never be enough food." She shook her head. "Never in the whole of his childhood was he held in loving arms, was he comforted for a scraped knee, was he made to feel loved or cherished. The women at this home told the children that their mothers were sinners and demons. Devil women, they said. And so Davey had terrible nightmares that he'd a tail growing through the back of his trousers, hard scales scabbing over his skin. Horns sprouting from his head. Twas an animal he believed himself to be, you see, Breda. Some terrible sinful creature. I s'pose he never quite stopped believing it."

Breda looked up at the shattered windows on the second floor, covered over in rusting bars. "How long did he live here?"

"Thirteen years. He was just about your age when he ran

away to London. Lived on the streets for a long time until he found work in a mechanic's that was steady enough. He lived in a room with four other boys who were as poor and alone as himself. Many years later, when he heard the home had burned, he returned to Ireland to see it for himself. To be sure twas really gone. And on the train down from Dublin to Lahinch, so the story goes, he met your grandmother. A dark-haired girl in a blue dress. They fell in love, married, and moved to her farm. Her parents weren't pleased—he was a boy from nowhere, with nothing. But he was a quick learner and he worked the land hard, and he gained her old father's respect. He was nearly forty-two by then, but sure twas the only real home he ever had. This is why he loves it so."

"What happened to her?" Breda asked softly. "My grand-mother."

"Well, when she was expecting your mother, they found the cancer in her body during a routine scan. She died before Maura took her first steps, God rest her." She sighed. "I don't know many things for sure, Breda, but if there's one, tis this: throwing your mother out is the single greatest regret of Davey's life."

Breda's heart was in her throat. She thought of all those little bodies buried just a few feet under, beneath the eroding clay. The meanness of the world where he'd grown up. The meanness of the *whole* world. A world where a new mother could be called a fallen woman and a person in search of a better life could be called an illegal alien, and people hurt each other again and again, not because they want to, but because they never learned another way. Why did it have to be like this? It was a question only Fionn Mac Cumhaill, who possessed all the wisdom of the universe, could answer.

"Mom can't come to him," Breda said, running a hand along the cold moss that clung to the charred stone wall. "If he dies, he'll die without ever seeing her again. They'll never get to make peace, or to say goodbye."

"Maybe not," Noeleen agreed, "but try to think of it like this: in Irish, we have a saying. Ar scáth a chéile a mhaireann an daoine. 'We live in each other's shadows.' Fathers and their daughters, Breda—those shadows cast long. Longer than an ocean. They always will. I have to believe, if we lose Davey, we lose him knowing that he loved his child. And that, for all their distance, she loves him back." She wiped her eyes. "I hope that gives you a bit more understanding of your old granddad. I know he can be a hard man at times. But Breda, believe me, he has such a good heart. Tis just so terribly difficult for him to let anyone see it."

"I believe you, Noeleen," Breda said quietly, remembering the picnic Granda had packed for the two of them, the bike he had given her, the way he'd whispered to Bo's mother so gently until her baby had been born.

"Well, I'm glad." Noeleen looked up at the burnt wreckage of the building one more time. "I'm very glad of that. Now. I s'pose we should be getting back to the hospital."

40.

WHEN THEY RETURNED TO TRALEE, Granda was still unconscious. They walked into his room, and Breda was stunned to find Tadgh sitting by his side, scrolling through his phone and sipping a cup of coffee.

"What are you doing here?" Noeleen demanded, placing two hands on her plump hips. "Tis one thing to be sitting out in the waiting room, but to be here at his *bedside*? The cheek! Just imagine if he woke up and saw *you*, of all people—"

"Noeleen." Breda put a hand gently on Noeleen's arm. "It's okay."

"Tis not. Davey would *not* like this, Breda. For a Fahey to see him in this state. For a *Fahey* to be holding vigil for him."

"Tadgh," said Breda, "could you excuse us for one second?"

"Course I can," said Tadgh. He got up and went into the hallway, closing the door softly behind him.

"Breda," Noeleen began, "I have to say, I don't like this one bit. That man may be your father, but it doesn't change the fact that he *wronged* your family. Your mother, and Davey, and, most of all, *you*."

"I know he did, okay?" Breda stared at Noeleen, who was standing across the bed from her, with Granda's body between them. "But what about the thing you just said to me? That we live in each other's shadows? Because you're right. I mean, I only met Tadgh this summer, but I've lived in his shadow all my life. And he's lived in mine. And my mom's and Granda's, too. And Granda has lived in his. And I guess we could all keep going with this whole not-speaking-about-it-and-pretending-it-will-go-away thing that everyone in this family is so good at, but with Granda lying here and us not knowing whether he'll live or die . . . I mean, wouldn't this be a good time to just, like, put it all to rest? For good?"

"But—"

"I'm not saying he's a good father. But he is *my* father. And I can see that he's trying, at least. So you don't have to like him or whatever, okay? I don't even know if *I* like him. But let's just . . . just try be nice to him for now. Okay?"

"Well, now." Noeleen gave Breda an embarrassed smile.

230

"Sometimes the chick knows more than the hen. You're right, of course. And I promise—I'll try."

"Thanks, Noeleen."

Noeleen reached out and held Breda in another tight hug.

"You know," she said, holding Breda at arm's length and looking her in the eyes, "I reckon you don't seem like the same girl you were when you stepped off that plane to come visit us."

"Well, that's good, I guess." Breda grinned. "Because I don't feel like that girl, either."

When Tadgh returned to Granda's room, Noeleen arranged her face in her best attempt at a genuine smile. "I'm off to the canteen to get a cup of tea," she said. "Would you like one, Tadgh?"

"I'm grand sure," he said, holding up his cup and trying to contain his surprise at the woman's sudden kindness. "I've got the coffee here. But I appreciate the offer."

As soon as she left the room, Tadgh turned to her and smiled. "Why do I get the feeling you—what's the American phrase?—went to bat for me?"

"This doesn't mean we're cool, you and me," Breda said. "It just means you're my blood, and blood stands up for blood. Granda taught me that."

"I'm your blood." Tadgh sipped his coffee, his cheeks flushing. "That's good enough for me."

❖ ❖ ❖

That evening, Dr. Philbin returned to examine Granda.

"He's still quite weak," the doctor said. "But he's fairly stable. If he regains consciousness in the next day or two, we'll be able to operate. He's certainly not out of the woods yet, though. So let's manage our expectations."

"What would you say his chances are now?" Tadgh asked.

"I'd say they've improved," the doctor said, his brow furrowing as he examined Granda's chart. "I'd say they're about fifty percent now."

Fifty-fifty. The toss of a coin. Noeleen pulled her rosary from her purse and began, again, to pray.

When night came, Tadgh went home to get some sleep, promising to return first thing in the morning. One of the nurses brought two foldable cots so that Noeleen and Breda wouldn't have to sleep in chairs again, but when Noeleen tried to stretch out across hers, it was too soft and it aggravated the pain in her back.

"Look, Noeleen," Breda said as the older woman struggled back into a seated position on the sagging cot. "Why don't you just go home, too? You drove all the way out to Liscannor today, and you didn't sleep at all last night. You can come back first thing in the morning."

"I won't leave you here alone," Noeleen said, though the bags under her eyes were purple and she couldn't get through a sentence without yawning. "And anyway, what if he wakes up and I'm not here?"

"He's not going to wake up," said the nurse who had just finished checking his vitals. "He might come round tomorrow or the next day, but at the moment, I suspect he is very far away." She looked between the two of them, her hands on her hips. "I've been doing this a long time, yeah? My opinion, you should *both* go home. You'll need your strength for what's ahead."

Noeleen nodded, gathering up her purse and her rosary beads, but Breda had already kicked off her shoes and sprawled her tall, thin body across the narrow cot. Before she left, Noeleen handed Breda her cell phone, an old flip model covered with dings and scratches.

"Take this," she said. "Ring me at home if anything changes."

Breda promised that she would, and no sooner had Noeleen left than she collapsed into a deep sleep, swirling with vivid dreams of cold stone hallways, mothers screaming for their children, and a little boy, skinny and pale, staring in terror as the claws grew from his body, transforming human hands into something monstrous.

41.

IT WAS DURING THIS DREAM THAT SHE heard someone speaking to her in a hushed voice. She was very far down inside the well of her dream and the voice was very weak. It called to her many times before she was able to swim back up to waking. When she did, and saw that she was still lying on her cot in the dim mechanical glow of the hospital room, she nearly jumped out of bed. Two blue disks hovered between all those machines. Two blinking blue disks. Granda's eyes—and they were open.

"Breda," he whispered. "Breda, my girl."

"Granda!" She jumped up and went to him, putting her arms gently around his frail body. "You're awake. The doctors said—"

234

"Ah, they don't know nothing. All that learning, and no sense." He winced, and sank back into his pillow.

"How are you feeling? Should I call the nurse?"

"Breda." His eyes fluttered, half closing. "Did I ever tell you the story of Tír na nÓg?"

She sat at the edge of his bed and smoothed his rumpled hair. "Granda, you need to rest. You can tell me another time. I'm going to hit the call button. The nurse should—"

"No." He shook his head. "That can wait. This cannot."

Of course there was no use arguing with Granda, even when he was lying broken in a hospital bed. And so he began, quietly and haltingly, to tell her one last story.

"Now, you remember Fionn Mac Cumhaill, Breda?"

"Of course I do. The greatest warrior of all time, who ate the Salmon of Knowledge."

"Good woman." He tried to sit up, winced in pain, and settled back into his pillow. "Well, after Fionn gained the wisdom of the universe, he grew up and became a man. He had a son, Oisín, who also became a famed warrior-poet, second only to his father. One day, Fionn and Oisín were deer hunting near the River Laune when a beautiful woman on a white horse approached them. She told them her name was Niamh, that she was the princess of the kingdom of Tír na nÓg, and that she had heard of Oisín's greatness and had come to take him back home to be her husband.

"Fionn knew this kingdom, for, of course, he knew *everything*, but Oisín did not. 'Tell me,' Oisín said to Niamh, 'what is your homeland like?'

"'It is the land of eternal youth,' she said. 'There is no pain in Tír na nÓg, and no suffering, and no one ever grows old.' Now, of course, who wouldn't want to live in such a place, Breda? A place so very different from the painful human world we know? And so, with his father's blessing, Oisín mounted Niamh's white horse and together they disappeared into the forest.

"Niamh was telling the truth—Tír na nÓg was truly a land of enchantment, and Oisín was very, very happy there with his new bride. But true happiness cannot last when we are away from those we love, and before long, Oisín yearned to return to Ireland to visit his father and the Fianna warriors, who he thought of as his brothers and sisters. Niamh agreed to lend him her white horse to take him there, but warned him that he must stay on the horse at all times, for if his feet touched Irish soil, he could never return again to his wife and the land of eternal youth.

"What she did not tell him was that time passed differently in Tír na nÓg than it does on earth. When Oisín returned to Ireland, he discovered that three hundred years had come and gone. The grand castle that had been his home was a crumbled ruin, and the village of his youth was filled with strangers. Worst of all, everyone he loved was long dead.

"His heart sinking, Oisín rode on through the Valley of the Thrushes, searching for some sign of the home he once knew. The land itself was as he remembered it—green and rocky and eternal—but what did that beauty matter without his family? At last, he came upon a band of men who were trying, without success, to move a large, smooth stone. Now remember, Breda, Oisín was still the strongest, greatest warrior in the land, second only to his father, and so he offered to help these men. Remembering Niamh's warning, he did not dismount his horse. Instead, he leaned down from his saddle and lifted the stone with one hand, as if it was no heavier than a pillow stuffed with goose feathers, and hurled it as far as he could throw. But when he did so, the saddle broke—and Oisín fell to the earth.

"In an instant, the white horse galloped away, and the band of men watched in horror as the powerful warrior shriveled up into the oldest, frailest man they had ever seen. They carried him to a nearby healer, but despite this holy man's powers, Oisín died that very night. Without his beloved wife to return to in Tír na nÓg, and without his father and warrior brothers and sisters in Ireland, he had no reason left to live."

The story was over, and Breda sat on the edge of Granda's

bed, listening to the hospital sounds, the beeping, and his breathing.

"Breda," he said.

"Yes, Granda?"

"I'm a very old man myself. I mightn't be quite three hundred years, but right now it certainly feels that way." He reached in the darkness for her hand. "But this summer, having you, my grandchild, live under my roof."

He paused, and took a ragged breath. "This summer, with you—this was my Tír na nÓg."

Breda held his hand, puffy and disfigured, against her cheek as her tears fell. "Granda," she whispered, "please don't leave me."

"I've been a pigheaded, silly old man," he went on. "But I love you, Breda. You know that, don't you?"

"I do." She nodded into his hand. "And I love you, Granda."

"Good," he said weakly. "That's very good to hear."

And through the rest of that long night, Breda kept her vigil at Granda's side, her hand curled around his, until the sun began to break over the mountains outside the hospital window.

42.

THE DOCTORS TOLD GRANDA HE WOULD need to remain hospitalized for at least a month, and he was still too weak to fight them on it. Noeleen packed herself a bag and moved to the farm with Breda. Together they drove up to Tralee and visited him every day. His progress was slow, but each day he grew a little stronger, slept a little less, ate a little more, watched a little more of the Irish-language dating show, *Paisean Faisean*, always pretending to hate it but always being annoyed if someone switched it off before the winning lad was announced. Two weeks into his convalescence, one of the hospital staff brought him a hamburger and baked bean dinner. He took one bite of the burger, spat it out, and accused the hospital of importing meat from the UK or, even worse, the United

States. "There is no way this dog food was produced by an Irish farmer!" he shouted in a reedy voice, throwing the limp sandwich back on the tray. "It tastes of nothing but pesticides and chemicals!" The hospital worker was horrified, but Breda and Noeleen beamed at each other across his bed—now they knew he was going to be okay.

By the beginning of August, Granda had made enough progress that his doctors cleared him to go home. It was a beautiful month, day after long, sunny day, but Granda was still confined mostly to his TV chair, which meant that Breda spent most of her time at home, too. Neighbors came and went constantly, helping out with the farming, dropping off groceries and hot meals, or simply sitting and keeping him company. Every Friday, Joe the butcher delivered fresh bacon and dirt-streaked vegetables from his garden—turnips, potatoes, carrots, and cabbage—and no matter how much Breda and Noeleen insisted, he wouldn't take any money. A few nights, JohnJoe, Jackie, Luke, and some other friends from Ballyglass brought the session to the farm, setting up in the sitting room, and though Granda smiled and nodded his head and tapped his slipper to the music, he was still too weak to perform as seanchaí.

Tadgh stopped by the farm nearly every day to visit with Breda and to check on the livestock. Granda was always polite, but he never invited Tadgh to stay for a cup of tea. But one morning, another sunny day at the end of August just a couple weeks before Breda was scheduled to fly home to Chicago, there was a knock on the door. Breda got up to answer it, as she always did.

"Sit down, girl," Granda ordered. "If a man can't answer the door at his own home, he's not a man a'tall."

"Granda, come on," Breda said. She was already halfway across the sitting room. "I've been answering the door for weeks now. It's not a big deal."

"Hand me my crutches, child."

Breda shook her head and sighed. There was no arguing with him. She walked over to the press, where his crutches were propped, and brought them over to his chair. She gripped his hands and held on as he slowly rose to standing, then crutched, at an achingly slow place, out of the sitting room toward the kitchen door. Breda followed close behind, in case he lost his balance.

When he opened the door, Tadgh was standing there with his hands behind his back and a huge smile on his face.

"Well?" demanded Granda. "Did you do it?"

"I did."

"Grand." Granda turned to Breda. "Come outside, now. We've something to show you."

Breda looked between her father and grandfather, but neither one of them said a word. They stepped slowly out of the house, not wanting to insult Granda by walking ahead of him, and crossed the driveway to where Tadgh's truck was parked. A small horse trailer was hitched to the back.

"Go on," Granda said, nodding at Breda. "Open it."

"Me?"

"Have I got another grandchild I might be speaking to?"

Breda's heart was pounding and she didn't know why. She stood on her tiptoes and unslid the heavy lock from its bolt. The metal door swung open. And there, inside, standing all by himself, was a brown calf with big, liquid eyes.

"Bo?" Breda whispered. The calf's ears twitched.

"All the lads down at the cattle mart will never let me live this one down," Granda said. He crossed his arms sternly, but his voice was soft. "I had to buy the little fella back for twice what I sold him."

"They had a good laugh, alright," Tadgh said, trying to hold back a smile.

"The things we do for our grandchildren." Granda shook his head. "They make us soft, so they do."

"Granda," Breda whispered. "Thank you."

"Ah, go on," he said, squinting out at the horizon.

Tadgh climbed up into the trailer and coaxed the little calf down the ramp. Together, the three of them led Bo down to the pasture where the herd was grazing in the sun. As Granda leaned against the stone fence, Tadgh unbolted the electric gate and gently pushed the calf into the field. The little creature had no sooner stepped through the gate when, on the far side of the field, his mother lifted her diamond-spotted head.

"Jaysus." Tadgh shook his head as she came galloping toward Bo. "I never in my life seen a cow run that fast."

"They'll be laughing at me for years about this one," Granda said, "and so they should, as you've made a right arse of me, Breda." But as he spoke, he absently reached down and stroked the top of Breda's head. She remained very still, suspecting that he was doing it without even realizing it, and as the ocean lapped just beyond the road, she stood between her dad and her granda and watched in quiet wonder the reunion of a parent with her child.

43.
SEPTEMBER

"**A**NGELS WERE MEANT TO FLY," GRUM-bled Granda. "Gannets. Rooks. Not humans."

"Granda, chill."

Breda reached up to stow his crutches in the overhead compartment and took her seat.

"Tis nothing more than an aluminium tube packed with human souls and rocketed into the sky." He eased himself slowly into his seat and pulled his seat belt across his waist. "Get the air hostess's attention, child. I'll need an old drop of whiskey if I'm to bear this journey."

"Granda, you can't order a *whiskey* right now. They're still helping people get seated."

"Excuse me, love," Granda called, leaning over to get the attention of the young woman in the green suit showing a mother how to buckle her toddler into the attached child belt. "How can a man get a whiskey around here?"

The flight attendant furrowed her carefully penciled brows at him. "Sir, I'm fairly busy at the moment."

"No respect for elders in this country anymore," he complained. "None a'tall!"

"It's his first time flying," Breda explained to the woman with a tight smile. "He's really nervous."

The flight attendant put her hands on her hips, looked down at the pair of them, and sighed. "I'll see what I can do."

Twenty minutes later, the engines roared to life and Granda swallowed the last of the brown liquor from his plastic cup.

"Man wasn't meant to fly, by God," he muttered, crushing the cup in his hand. "That's the realm of angels."

"It will be just fine, I promise."

"Now *there's* a Yank attitude if I ever saw one—thinking you know more than God himself. The arrogance!"

Breda took the bait and kept up the argument as long as she could, to keep him distracted. It only worked until the plane accelerated down the runway and lurched into the early autumn sky. Granda gasped and squeezed his eyes shut, clutching his swollen fingers, and began to pray, loudly. Breda leaned over his lap to look at Ireland from above, its glittering patchwork of green.

"Granda," she said softly. "You have to see this."

"Why?" he shouted, squeezing his eyes shut tighter. "It's going down, is it?"

"Granda. Open your eyes."

One crinkled eye grudgingly fluttered open, then the other. His head swiveled slowly to the small glass oval. His eyes widened.

"By God," he said, craning his neck to stare out the window at the land below. "Tis some country, in't it?"

Breda put her head on his shoulder. "Tis, Granda."

And as the plane hurtled toward Chicago, an old man and his granddaughter watched the wide Atlantic ripple below them, shimmering in the sun like the scales of some magnificent fish.

Acknowledgments

I T WAS SARA CROWE WHO FIRST SUGGESTED that I try writing a book for younger readers. And, Sara, you were right. Working on Breda's story is what got me through some of the darkest parts of 2020. Deep gratitude to you and all the Pips.

Thank you to the top-notch team at Quill Tree Books, most of all to my brilliant editor and friend, Alexandra Cooper. Alex, thank you for always seeing my first drafts for what they could be, and helping me to get them there. Heartfelt thanks to the other members of the editorial team at Quill Tree, particularly Rosemary Brosnan and Allison Weintraub. Thank you to Alexandra Rakaczki for your keen eye and attention to detail. Thank you to Devin Elle Kurtz for the stunning cover art, Kathy Lam for the beautiful interior pages and jacket design, and Erin Fitz-simmons for your art direction. Thank you to Emily Mannon, Jacquelynn Burke, Patty Rosati, Mimi Rankin, Katie Dutton, Kristen Eckhardt, and James Neel for your hard work helping this book find its way to readers. And Jenny Sheridan, my fellow Chicago girl: thank you for always being such an incredible advocate for my work!

As usual, this book required far more research than I'd originally planned; luckily, I had several excellent teachers. Martin Healy had me covered on horses, Gerard Doherty on sheep, and Denis Foley and Paddy Crowley on cows. I must give a special thank-you to Paddy for patiently answering my many, many questions about calving. I hope we all get a night out in Killarney (or even better, Barraduff) very soon. Go raibh math agat to Caroline Póil, for answering my questions about your beautiful and complicated native language. Finally, thank you to my parents. Without your loving (and free!) babysitting services, I would be truly lost.

An excellent book that helped me expand my learning about Dingle's natural wonders is *Ireland: A Smithsonian Natural History*. I'm also grateful to the Blasket Centre/Ionad an Bhlascaoid—a stunning and fascinating museum that I've been lucky to visit several times over the last few years, which helped me to deepen my understanding and appreciation of Blasket Islands history.

Finally, thank you to my husband, Denis, and the entire Foley family. Warm days at Inch, windy days on Banna and Glenbeigh; searching for jellyfish along the strand in Caherdaniel; spotting stray cats on the path to Kenmare; wandering around the completely guestless (and now closed) hotel at Glencar; the baptisms of our daughters at Saint Mary's Cathedral; Taytos and blackcurrant at Páidí O Sé's; lobster in Waterville; turbot at the Parknasilla; visiting the graves of our forebears at Muckross and Keel and Ardfert; drives through the majestic Conor Pass; getting lost on the Ring of Beara and then returning, unwillingly, into Glengarriff and civilization; the Black Valley in the rain; Valentia in the cloudless blue; music at the Grand and the Fáilte and yes, even McSorley's; afternoon visits with Jackie Farmer; and most of all, climbing Ballaugh Hill together, first just the two of us, and later, with our children— these are some of the greatest memories of my life. My favorite thing about the Kingdom is it gave me you.